Within

Clare C. Marshall

Cover by David Farrell
Woulds & Shoulds Editing and Design
http://editinganddesign.com

Images by Shutterstock.com

ISBN-13: 978-0-9877794-0-3

PROLOGUE

Harry's corner was the intersection between Spring Garden Road and Dresden Row, right next to the Shoppers Drug Mart. He jingled his Tim Horton's cup at the exiting patrons of the drug store, and they'd shake their heads at him, or pretend he wasn't there. He'd wish them a happy day anyway. What went around came around, and if he gave enough cheer despite the emptiness of his cup every morning and night, maybe, someday, God might cut him a break.

The sun had set three hours ago, but Harry decided to stick to his spot anyway. Sometimes the other fellas came at night and wanted to stand on his corner, sayin' they were the night watch, but Harry held firm. It was his place, and it wasn't as bad as some of those other corners in Halifax. Sometimes, especially on Wednesdays, as the drunken teenagers and university students stumbled back to Dalhousie campus, they would pat him on the shoulder and stuff leftover change from their cheap drinks at the Dome into his cup. Those were good nights.

He waited for that to happen, jingling his cup to keep him company. Weren't many folks out that night. Too early for the students. But Harry was patient. He had no family to go home to, or a home to go home to for that matter.

The streets were quiet until Harry spotted three figures walking side by side down Spring Garden. It was dark, and Harry's eyes weren't too good anymore, but he noticed that they wore identical black robes that hid their faces and their hands. He caught brief glances of their sandaled feet as they scraped across the sidewalk.

They didn't look like they had wallets, or pockets, but Harry shook his cup at them anyway. "Spare some change, misters?"

The men didn't stop. Like giant birds, they extended their arms and swept over him, catching him in the fabric of their robes. Harry held on tightly to his cup and its precious change as the silk wrapped around him, swallowing him. He tried to fight his way out.

"What are you doing? What's going—?"

Harry grunted as something sharp drove into his lower back. The blade twisted, sending an intense ripple of pain up his right side. His arms went limp. The change he had worked so hard to earn clanged once more as it hit the sidewalk and then went silent. When he tried to cry out, more fabric was stuffed in his mouth. A pool of his blood formed on the pavement as he was half carried, half dragged away.

CHAPTER ONE

"Could you tell me what happened?"

Ellie fidgeted in her seat and didn't look Dr. So in the eye. Her hair hadn't been brushed recently, and little blond-brown pieces rebelled from her scalp and stuck up like she'd been electrocuted. The hour had just started; it was going to be a long session. "I don't want to be here."

The school counsellor didn't respond. After nearly twenty years, he was used to the resistance that teens showed toward expressing their feelings, especially after a traumatic event. It took time to accept what happened, and in this case, it would take a lot of work for Ellie Emerson to realize that what happened to Trinity was not her fault. The unconscious—if such a mechanism did exist—was a powerful force, and hated to see the conscious mind suffer. He lifted his Citadel High mug, fresh hot coffee steaming from the top, and let it hover before his lips.

"That's fine, Ellie. Let's talk about Trinity. Tell me about her."

Dr. So knew that it wasn't the best question he could've asked, but he was determined to accomplish something within the hour. Ellie repeatedly clasped and unclasped the fabric of the couch.

"You knew her," she grumbled.

"You knew her best," Dr. So replied.

"Not really."

"Who knew her better?"

"Probably Zack."

"Her boyfriend." Dr. So paused. "But I'm asking about your relationship with Trinity, not his."

"What does it matter?" Ellie spat. Her eyes were red from crying, and her voice wavered with the mention of Trinity's name. "She's ... Trinity is..."

Dr. So leaned forward in his chair. This could be it. "Tell me what happened that night, Ellie."

Ellie drew in a deep breath through puckered lips, as if sucking in all of the oxygen in the room would stop her from bursting into tears again. She bit her trembling lip and began.

"We were finishing up a school project at my mom's house..."

*

It started to rain just as they were leaving Ellie's mother's house in Lawrencetown. The clouds had threatened to relieve themselves earlier in the day but instead they hovered over the greater Halifax area, stretching towards the Eastern Shore. The longer they waited, the wetter the roads would be, and the longer it would take to drive Zack and Trinity back to Halifax.

Ellie was pleased with the delay, and planted her feet firmly in the kitchen. Zack gravitated towards the door, with Trinity not far behind. That was the way it always was with them. Attached at the arm, or the hip, or both. Trinity had this classic beauty about her that had recently become plastic to Ellie. Ever since she started dating Zack last year, she started wearing more eye make-up, especially on the days that she and Zack were going to spend time with each other after school. Her eyes were a dark blue, so pure that Ellie used to be jealous of them, back in seventh grade when they were just starting to become aware of their bodies. Most people would say that Trinity's hair was black, but it was really a burnt coffee brown. Ellie had cut her hair on a sleepover a few years ago, back when they used to whisper and giggle about all the cute boys in the class. Now all Trinity whispered about was Zack, and Ellie knew she kept the details to herself—something she both appreciated and resented.

"Here's the list I made of things we have to do tomorrow before the presentation," Trinity said, pulling out a folded piece of loose leaf from her jeans pocket.

She placed it in Zack's waiting hand. His skin was darker than Trinity's—that wasn't hard—but Ellie knew it was partly because Zack got a lot of sun, when he went for his run every morning. Of course, Ellie was never there to see him run, except in gym class, but she knew about it. His arms and his legs were toned—not too muscled—but perfect, not too intimidating for someone like Ellie who did her one hundred sit-ups and push-ups every night. She noticed how Trinity's fingers lingered and caressed his as Zack opened the note.

"Well, aren't you a keener," he said, smiling.

Trinity returned his smile. "I try."

He bent to kiss her on the forehead. Ellie looked away. Zack had been so good all night, keeping Trinity at arm's length, focusing on the project and enjoying Ellie's conversation. All that, ruined with one kiss. She shouldn't have gotten her hopes up. She gathered their presentation for tomorrow—a piece of white Bristol board rolled neatly, thanks to Zack—and opened the nearby closet door to fetch their coats.

She stole a glance at them. He was still lost in Trinity's eyes.

"We'd better get going before this rain gets worse," she said, focusing her attention on the car outside.

Zack and Trinity detached themselves. Ellie threw their coats on the now-bare kitchen table—they could sort that out themselves. She took her time crossing the room again, drinking up Zack with her eyes as she passed—his almond eyes, his dark hair, his body, his cologne hanging in the air wherever he stood—she hoped it lingered long enough for her to bask in it when she got back. Zack shared a secret smile with Trinity as they zipped up their coats.

Ellie opened the front door and beelined for the car with the rolled up Bristol board for their English project under their arm. The car—her mother's 2010 Toyota Corolla—was unlocked. She shoved herself into the driver's seat and threw the Bristol board and her purse in the back. She regretted her harsh treatment of the project seconds afterward, and twisted around to arrange it more neatly before Zack could see.

Zack and Trinity, hand in hand, followed. Trinity made sure the door was locked, even though Ellie's mother was upstairs, reading. Ellie scolded herself for not thinking of that. More points for Trinity. Ellie noticed how Zack pulled Trinity closer to him as the raindrops intensified and smothered them. Ellie felt sick to her stomach.

"Shotgun!" Trinity screamed as she rushed for the front passenger's side, her voice going from muffled to loud as she opened and slammed the door.

"Damn it!" Zack said as he climbed into the backseat. "Foiled again."

Yes, foiled again, and again, and again, Ellie thought as she started the car.

Lawrencetown was about a forty-five minute drive from Halifax. Usually Ellie didn't go to her mother's house during the week, but her father was away in Sydney on business for a few days. She could've easily gone to either Zack or Trinity's, since they lived in the Quinpool area in Halifax, but Ellie's mother was eager to repay Zack and Trinity for all the times they had hosted Ellie at their houses for supper. That was before they'd heard about the storm warning.

The rain pelted the windshield like rapid gunfire. Just as the wipers swept it clean, it was replaced by more splattering blots. The trees and the road blurred together like an impressionist painting in the dark. It would be a long ride home, with Trinity in the front and Zack in the back. She stole glances at him in the rear-view mirror, and then flicked on the radio.

"Halifax's streets are slowly emptying due to a string of disappearances of the homeless..."

Ellie turned down the volume. "News. Boring. There's gotta be some CDs in this car."

"Yeah, I didn't bring my iPod, otherwise I woulda hooked it up when we got in," Zack replied.

Trinity dug around in the side pockets of the car and retrieved some of the discs. "We got Metric, Joel Plaskett, and the Nitty Gritty Dirt Band? I didn't know you liked country!"

"Pretty sure that's my mom's," Ellie muttered. "Put in Metric, I guess."

Trinity slid the Metric CD in its spot, cutting off the news announcer. So what, the homeless were missing, who cared. Cleaner streets meant safer streets. The song Empty strummed softly and provided a momentary distraction from the rain firing on the windshield.

"Should probably call your 'rents, Trin," Zack said.

"Yeah, yeah." She reached awkwardly into the pockets of her tight jeans, her hands coming out empty. "Hmm. Must be in my purse?"

"It's back here. You want me to…?"

"Nah, I got it," Trinity said.

Ellie glanced over as Trinity unbuckled her seatbelt. The little signal thing on her dashboard started blinking and making warning sounds.

"Hurry up. This rain is making me nervous enough," Ellie said.

"It's all right, Ell, I'm fine."

Trinity reached for her purse on the floor of the backseat. Even in the darkness of the rear-view mirror, Ellie saw Zack reach out his hand to Trinity. A small, secret smile that she wasn't supposed to see crawled across his face. She had no doubt that Trinity returned it as she squeezed his hand.

Zack saw it first.

"Ellie, watch out!"

Ellie's eyes snapped from the mirror to the windshield. It looked like a giant looming monster, with two blaring yellow headlights for eyes and a roaring bear-like horn; before Ellie had time to swerve, the mechanical beast crashed headfirst into her. The impact immediately triggered the driver's seat airbags. After the whiplash, the world was a blur as Ellie's head slammed onto the steering wheel, knocking her out cold.

*

It would have been easier for them to go to Trinity's house to do the project.

"Ellie's mom…she's…not the nicest person in the world," Trinity warned Zack gently as they waited for Ellie outside the school. Trinity was wearing her dark blue low-rise jeans and a v-neck purple and pink t-shirt, covered by her white hoodie that Zack had bought her last Christmas. The wind tussled her black hair as she gave him a quick kiss on the cheek.

"What do you mean?" he asked.

Trinity checked the school entrance to make sure Ellie wasn't nearby. "I don't think she treats Ellie that well."

"Like...she's physically abusive?"

"No...that's not what I mean..." Trinity sighed and crossed her arms. "You'll see, maybe."

Zack drew her into his arms and ran his fingers through her silky smooth hair. "Ellie would tell you if something was up though, right?"

"Yeah, I guess."

He could see Ellie walking down the pathway towards the cars, where they were standing. She carried three different pieces of Bristol board rolled into one, a binder overflowing with loose papers in one hand, not to mention the sagging backpack slung over one shoulder. As she got closer Zack could see the tiny beads of sweat forming on her forehead, but Ellie's face was set with determination. Trinity broke free from him and ran towards Ellie.

"Here, let me take that," she said, and before Ellie could protest, Trinity took the heavy binder into her arms. "Jeesh. What do you have in here?"

"Extra homework. I've decided to do that optional chemistry project, for bonus points. Just in case I didn't do as well as I thought on the midterm." Ellie smiled as she approached Zack. "Hey."

"Hi," he replied, and offered to take the Bristol board from her. She seemed extremely relieved at this, even though it was the lightest thing she was carrying.

After stuffing their bags into Ellie's mother's car, they headed out of the city to Lawrancetown. Trinity had called shotgun so he was feeling lonely in the backseat. The girls chatted away in the front about girl things. Trinity occasionally stuck her hand back, and he gave it a squeeze to reassure her that he was still there. It took them a little longer than usual to get out of the city because it was the beginning of rush hour, and both bridges were starting to be backed up.

"You sure we shouldn't go to my house?" he asked Ellie, leaning forward as much as his seatbelt would allow.

She glanced at him in the rear-view mirror. She had a cheery look on her face, and didn't seem to mind the slow movement of the traffic. "My mom says she'll cook dinner. I know it's kind of a long way, but you guys can always stay the night if you have to and I can drive us to school in the morning."

Zack had to suppress a smile. The idea of spending the night with Trinity was too tempting. They had already agreed to save themselves until after graduation, which was at least two months away, but there had been a couple of times that they'd been so close to forgetting that promise. No. Zack slowly leaned back as he banished those wonderful feelings and thoughts from his mind. Not at Ellie's house. That would just be...weird.

"Maybe on the weekend we could do that," Trinity suggested. She was probably thinking the same thing he was, hell, maybe she was even getting turned on by it. This excited him. He spent the rest of the trip with his hands over the front of his jeans, hoping that Ellie's view in the rear-view mirror wasn't on his crotch.

Ellie's mother—Ms. Beverly Emerson—had made dinner, but only the salad. She had ordered two large pizzas, which were keeping warm in the oven. She greeted Zack and Trinity warmly, as Ellie rushed downstairs to dump things in her bedroom. Beverly Emerson was dolled up in large clip-on earrings and lipstick too red for her complexion, but she seemed very interested in what he and Trinity were planning for their future.

"We've both been accepted to Dalhousie," Trinity told her with a polite smile. Zack squeezed her hand and felt a hint of pride. They were going to share their entire lives together, he knew it. This was only the beginning for them.

"I would like for Ellie to go to Dalhousie, but she's applied for Acadia and that other university. In Antigonish. What's it called…?"

"Saint F.X.," Zack supplied.

"Yes, that." Beverly shook her head. "She just wants to get away from me, I know it."

Ellie thumped up the stairs with the Bristol board in hand as Trinity shook her head, and said in her politest voice, "I'm sure she'll miss you if she does."

"Hmmph." Beverly acknowledged her daughter with a curt hello and gestured to the oven. "Whenever you're ready to eat, honey, there's pizza in there."

"You told us that twice," Ellie muttered.

Beverly seemed to ignore Ellie's comment and instead flashed another smile at Trinity and Zack. "I'll be upstairs in my study if you need me. Just save some pizza for me."

After she left the kitchen, Ellie unfurled the Bristol board on the kitchen table like a giant map. "Sorry about my Mom, she's kinda weird," Ellie said with a half-smile to Zack.

He shrugged and thought about what Trinity had told him earlier. Under the table, Trinity put her hand on his leg. He patted her hand gently, but here was not a good place to get a boner. "She's all right."

"That's 'cause you're a cute guy with a bright future," Ellie replied as she fetched three plates from the cupboard above the stove.

Zack grinned. "Well, you gotta appreciate a woman who can recognize—"

Trinity smacked him hard in the arm, with a look of pretend horror on her face. "Zackary Sato!"

17

"Yeah? What?"

Ellie's cheeks flushed a deep red, and she quickly changed the subject. "Anyone hungry?"

After scarfing down their pizza, they put their greasy fingers to work on their English project. They had to choose one of the three Shakespeare plays they'd sped through that semester and make a newspaper article about one of the events that happened in the story. Both Ellie and Trinity had desperately wanted to do Romeo and Juliet, and even though Zack was leaning towards Hamlet, he let the ladies win and racked his brain for Shakespeare-esque wordplay. They had already written up the article a few days ago in class, and now they had to assemble it on the Bristol board.

Ellie measured and cut out light brown pieces of brown Bristol board to give the illusion of old newspaper while Trinity wrote out the article in large letters on the cutouts. Zack had drawn the scene where Romeo slays Tybalt, which was what the article was about. He mounted it on one of the cut outs and pasted it in the middle of the board.

"So who wants to read the article tomorrow?" Ellie asked, breaking a long silence.

Zack shrugged. "If you guys don't want to, I will."

The corners of Trinity's lips lifted in a silent thank you. She didn't like public speaking.

"Okay," Ellie said, fixing her hair behind her ears. "I'll introduce the project and talk about why we chose Romeo and Juliet, blah blah blah, and you can read the article."

"Sounds good."

"And I'll be Vana White," Trinity said, leaping up and curtsying to Zack with a devilish look in her eye.

Zack pictured Trinity in a revealing sparkling dress—no, no, stop that. He glanced at Ellie instead and made a joke about how wrong it would be for him to be Vana White. That brought a genuine smile to her face and Trinity's hand returned danger-ously close to his crotch.

It only took about three hours for them to finish. By then, it was getting dark and the rain clouds were coming in. Zack rolled the project up and placed it near the front door.

"We should probably be getting home soon. What with the drive and these nasty looking clouds," Zack said, looking out the front window.

"Yeah…soon," Ellie agreed slowly.

They stayed in the kitchen for another twenty minutes or so, cleaning up their mess. Zack grabbed another slice of pizza and Trinity squeezed his ass when Ellie wasn't looking. What had gotten into her tonight? He had to be careful. He was starting to like it. But if he liked it too much…

The rain came, pelting on the windows, and that's when Zack was ready to go. They might have time for a quick make-out session in his basement, but only if they left in the next few minutes. Otherwise it would be getting too late.

While Ellie had her back turned to gather their coats from the closet, he and Trinity stole a moment of alone time. She was practically ready to jump him and he could barely deny her. Her full, delicious lips brushed against his ear.

"Come stay at my house tonight," she whispered.

Her words washed over him like cold water after a hot shower. "Your parents would kill me."

"Not if we wake up earlier than them. My mom's so busy with—"

"We'd better go before the rain gets worse," Ellie said.

Zack snapped out of Trinity's eyes as Ellie marched for the door. Had she heard them? Not that it really mattered. Trinity probably told Ellie lots of things, being her best friend and all…but Zack couldn't help but feel awkward as he watched Ellie dive into the car, rain plastering her hair to her face.

The time between that moment and the moment of the accident was blurry and on fast-forward. He remembered Trinity's deep blue eyes gazing into his as he squeezed her hand—her touch was warm and soft. And then, the headlights, searing into his eyes so fiercely that he had to look away from his beautiful girlfriend. He had only a split second to shout a warning to Ellie, who was watching him in the rear-view mirror.

"Ellie, watch out!"

Zack's body slammed against the back seat so hard that all of the air was pushed out of his lungs. His seatbelt held him firmly in place. He sucked in the air greedily, his chest aching, and opened his eyes.

The airbag activated on Trinity's side, but she wasn't there to feel the impact. Caught in an awkward position between the front and back seats, she smashed through the back windshield, flew ten feet in the air and landed head first onto the cold, wet pavement.

In that first moment, all he felt was shock. One second, Trinity was here, holding his hand, and the next…she was zipping by him, with no way for him to save her. With trembling hands, Zack unbuckled his seatbelt. Ellie's forehead was on the steering wheel. Out cold. Trinity's cell phone stuck out of her purse like a beacon. Zack grabbed it and dialled 911. It rang two or three times before someone answered. Wasn't someone supposed to answer immediately? He kicked open the passenger door with both feet and tumbled out into the rain.

"This is 911 emergency. How can I assist you?"

"Please…help." Zack had to shout over the rain. He squinted. The front of the truck that had smashed into Ellie's car was completely wrecked. It was dark and the rain blinded him but he didn't see any sign of the driver. He gave a choppy description of their location and what had happened, but his mind was on

Trinity. Her body was about ten feet away. The wind howled and prevented him from going too far too fast. The woman from 911's voice disappeared after a while, and Zack dropped the cell phone in favour of using hands to crawl along the pavement to reach Trinity. He barely felt the tiny rocks that embedded in his bleeding hands and knees. He was so very tired. Each step was more awkward than the last, and he felt his hearing leave him as darkness started to settle in.

Blood and something not-blood poured from a wound on Trinity's head, but all Zack could do was collapse beside her. She stared vacantly passed him. He felt a sob well up in his throat but there seemed to be too much water everywhere already. The last things he remembered were blue and red flashing lights and men in light blue jumpers running for him. *Save her*, he thought he said, but what he really wanted to say was *let me die too*.

*

Fuck it was raining hard. The wipers were beating the windshield at maximum speed but Jasper couldn't see shit. He shouldn't have agreed to do the run. One of the other brethren could've done it easy enough. Easier even. Now he was stuck out in the middle of the highway in this giant truck that Edmund had rented for him, just for a pitiful pile of human remains. Why couldn't they have just left them in the cave? It wasn't like anyone else knew about that place, right?

Jasper put more pressure on the gas pedal, and hydroplaned for a moment before regaining control. He had to get this job done as fast as possible. Just being on this road alone gave him the creeps.

Through the rain he saw a pair of blurry headlights. He

floored it. That could be the cops, on patrol. He wasn't going that fast. Sixty, seventy, maybe? Nope, over a hundred.

He was about to break when he hit another puddle and the wheels spun out of control. The headlights were bigger now but he was close enough to see it wasn't a cop car. The car smashed head-on into the front of the truck. The bottom of the steering wheel dug into Jasper's beer gut; that and his tight seat belt kept him from going anywhere.

At first he didn't know what to do. Get the ashes? They were in the dash. He had cargo in the back: boxes stuffed with packing material, decoys in case he got stopped by the police. He hastily unbuckled his seatbelt and reached for the dash. His hands were shaking, and cold. He climbed over the seat and retrieved the wooden box. The whole thing was designed to be biodegradable. Opening the passenger door, he climbed out of the truck with the box tucked under his arm.

Unfortunately, the box hadn't been properly sealed. Upon hitting the ground, the ashes—which the brethren had painstakingly burned and ground into a fine powder—blew up in his face and all over the road. He spit and wiped his eyes, the box clattering to the pavement.

Oh fuck.

Someone was lying on the pavement some feet away, a girl he thought. The driver, also a girl, was unconscious at the wheel. Someone—a guy—was climbing out of the back. He dashed for the ditch and slid in, his pants caking with mud.

Fuck this was bad. Screw the ashes. Rain could take care of them poor souls. Edmund wouldn't he happy about that, but he was getting the fuck out of there. Jasper thought he could hear sirens in the distance as he fled into the trees.

*

Ellie didn't remember becoming conscious again, but she did remember leaning against Zack's wet t-shirt. He was holding an ice pack to her forehead. They were sitting side by side on some sort of bench, and Ellie felt motion around her, as if they were moving at top speed.

"What...?" But before she could get the question out, the scene came back to her in hazy, half-remembered images. Lights. Rain. Crash. Blinding pain in her forehead.

"You all right?"

It wasn't Zack's voice. It was a paramedic, sitting across from them. He was a middle aged man with black hair, which was plastered to his skull from the rain. They were in the back of an ambulance, Ellie realized. It was dim, with most of the lighting coming from the back door windows. There was only one person missing from the vehicle.

"Where's Trinity?" she managed to say.

Zack averted his eyes, and Ellie realized his face was puffed up, as if he had been crying.

"Your friend is in the other ambulance. Everything is going to be all right," the paramedic assured her. "You have a concussion—"

"Other ambulance?" Ellie interrupted. If she wasn't with them in this ambulance, wouldn't that mean she needed more intensive care?

Oh no. No...she couldn't bear to think it. Was Trinity...dead?

"What happened to her?" she demanded.

"We're going to get her to the hospital," the paramedic replied. "I know it's difficult, but—"

"Zack. What happened to her?"

He didn't say anything. He was far away, and Ellie couldn't reach him. Was he ignoring her on purpose? She was the driver.

That meant it was her fault. The thought struck sharply in her gut and hurt almost as much as her throbbing head.

But the truck slammed into them. That didn't make it Ellie's fault...right? And the car! Her mother was going to kill her. If Trinity was dead, or worse, a vegetable because of her, it wouldn't matter anyway. She'd never forgive herself. Zack would never forgive her either.

*

"Thank you, Ellie," Dr. So said. "Our session is up. You made real progress today."

Ellie jumped to her feet, avoiding the counsellor's eye and heading directly for the door. Progress? No, there was no progress. She'd just relived the moment that destroyed her life. Trinity's life. Ellie had no one to blame but herself.

And Zack.

Her stomach knotted as she threw open the counsellor's door, and slammed it shut again.

CHAPTER TWO

Zack's surroundings didn't matter to him anymore. The past few days were a blur, a mixture of waiting and bad hospital food. He and Ellie were rushed to the hospital in a separate ambulance than Trinity. Despite a few cuts and bruises, and being scared out of their fucking minds, they were fine. Ellie stayed for a night in the hospital, and then her father came back from Sydney and took her home. Zack refused to leave the hospital, however, until he knew what happened to Trinity.

Trinity was given her own room at the QEII Hospital, and no one was allowed to see her for what seemed like eternity. Mr. and Ms. Hartell—or Stephanie and George, as they insisted—hovered in the waiting room like nervous bees and stung any doctor or medical-looking person that walked by, demanding information before the meds made some excuse to get away. As Trinity's parents, he guessed they had the right to do that.

Zack sat quietly, pretending to read a three-year-old copy of Cosmo. The glossy pages were a blur as he thumbed through the sex advice (and had a gut-wrenching realization that he wouldn't need that anymore, no, he could never imagine being with anyone else, not ever) and the fashion photo shoots (Trinity never really liked fuchsia, she liked black and blue and sometimes green and red) while waiting for the doctor came out. All he could see, over and over, was Trinity flying through the back windshield, the glass shattering everywhere. He tried not to imagine the sound of her skull cracking against the pavement. Tried not to imagine his life without her. No Trinity at graduation. No Trinity at Dalhousie University. Trinity gone, forever.

He leaned back in his chair, shutting his eyes. If he could hold her in his mind, he could bring her to life there, relive their memories together there. Grow old there...

His eyes were heavy with the want of sleep, and so he surrendered. The magazine fell from his fingers to the floor, and Zack dreamed.

*

It had taken him days to work up the courage to ask her out. It was grade eleven, and he and Trinity shared a math class. She sat in front of him, which gave him occasion to stare at her hair, shiny and black, and to smell the fragrant hairspray that kept it so perfect. She wore it down most of the time, but at certain angles he could see the curve of her neck. Sometimes she turned her head and glanced at him through a cage of long eyelashes and half-moon eyes.

They had talked, a few times, but it was mostly about assignments and homework. He knew that she lived across the Commons, maybe a few streets from where his family lived. But as soon as the bell rang, she was out the door before he could get a chance to gather his stuff.

One day, he raced through the class assignment to pack up five minutes early. He felt ridiculous, sitting there with his hands clasped over his stacked math book and binder while everyone around him was scribbling lazily on their loose leaf. He couldn't even check his phone, as there was a strict no cell phone policy during class time. Instead, he slouched in his chair and traced the deep notches already carved into his desk with his pencil, keeping his eyes fixed on Trinity. Today she was wearing a cute vintage-looking white and blue polka dot top, sleeveless, with little frills on the shoulders. The hair on her arm rose slowly and Zack could see the little goosebumps forming on her flesh. He tugged at his hoodie, wishing he could wrap it around—

"Zackary Sato."

His eyes flicked up to the teacher, Ms. Lewis, a stout, generally well-mannered woman who rarely raised her voice. She held a piece of chalk in her left hand and there was a fresh equation on the board that hadn't been there a few minutes ago.

"Uh...yes?" Zack sat up in his chair and haphazardly opened his math book to a random page.

"You look like you're ready to go somewhere," Ms. Lewis said, folding her arms.

Some of the class turned to look at him, including Trinity. All the embarrassment he had felt faded. It was worth it to have her look at him, for her to know who he was.

"You only have a minute or two to get this homework equation down before the bell rings for lunch," she continued, gesturing to the board. "Then I'm erasing it."

Zack scrambled to open his binder but he had even less time than Ms. Lewis had said. The bell rang and everyone—namely, Trinity—was up and on their way out the door. Zack wrote down the equation as fast as he could, without looking down at the quality of his work, while keeping his Trinity in his periphery. She slipped through the torrent of people clogging up the doorway, and disappeared into the hallway.

He scooped up his books and binders and slung his backpack over his shoulder. Whether or not he copied the equation down correctly, Zack didn't know or care. She would not escape him today.

Out in the crowded hallway, filled with rowdy teenagers storing their things in their lockers, all making their way down the hall to the cafeteria, he spotted her. She was walking confidently—in small black heels, Zack noted—in the opposite direction of the teenage traffic, towards a group of six lockers and a set of stairs about ten feet from him. He headed towards her but was blocked again by a flood of Oceanography students pouring out of the classroom directly across from the math room. Like a drowning man he gasped for air and peaked between the students' heads—and no, she wasn't going for the lockers! She was going down the stairs!

Zack nudged his way through the crowd, not caring who he disturbed. If she went down those stairs without him seeing where she was going, it would be another day that she was lost to him.

But then, coming up the stairs with another group of students, a girl with short blonde hair wearing a red and yellow scarf around her neck stopped Trinity. She said something to her, but Trinity tried to move away, and so the girl grabbed her arm. It wasn't an unfriendly gesture, but Trinity seemed mildly annoyed. It gave him the time to weave his way towards them, and to work up his nerve to actually speak to the girl of his dreams.

He'd been in debt to Ellie ever since.

"Ellie, stop it, I have to get in line for lunch."

"Why? That meeting isn't today, is it?"

"Yeah, it is."

"No, it's tomorrow at lunch, I'm pretty sure."

Zack felt invisible to her again. He wouldn't be the awkward creepy guy in this scenario; no, he refused to be silent any longer around her. "What meeting?"

Her eyelashes, heavy with mascara, flickered up and revealed her beautiful blue irises, her pupils narrowing in the light from the windows in the classroom behind him.

"Scrapbooking club," she said, with a small embarrassed smile. "I…I'm thinking of quitting though. It's eating up my allowance." Her very presence was making him smile like a crazy goof, even though there wasn't really anything funny about it all. In his periphery, Ellie gave him a tiny wave but her voice seemed so far away. "I'm Ellie. I don't think I've met you before…?"

"Yeah, I'm Zack. And uh, I'm in math class with Trinity," he replied, pointing at her and lightly grazing her arm. Even though the touch had barely lasted a millisecond he felt the air on his arms rise.

"Oh! You look kind of familiar…" Ellie's lips and nose scrunched up as she examined Zack's face. He felt himself blush. There were quite a few Asians that went to Citadel High, but he stood apart because only his mother was Japanese. He had inherited the Asian eyes and hair, but the rest of his face—his Roman nose, the higher than normal cheekbones, a few freckles that spotted the skin under his eyes—that was all his white, Canadian-born father.

Zack was about to make a joke about his racial background when Ellie's face lit up. "You won that digital art award last year, right?"

"Uh, yeah, actually I did." It felt like so long ago now, and so little an accomplishment. His dad had framed the certificate and nailed it to Zack's bedroom wall, but really all he got it for was because the rest of the people in his Tech class in grade ten barely knew what Photoshop—much less Indesign—were. They had probably thought the course was a typing class or some other bird course. The fact that she actually remembered him receiving that award made him feel vaguely uncomfortable, yet at the same time, it was kind of impressive.

"I think I was in that class with you," she said with a shrug, as if answering the unspoken is-she-a-stalker? question.

"It sounds like you know a lot about design. Maybe you should come with us to the Scrapbooking meeting," Trinity suggested, curling a piece of her straight black hair around her ear. "If you're not busy."

"No, no, nope, not busy." The words tripped and fell out of Zack's mouth and he quickly wiped his chin, to make sure no drool had accompanied them. He didn't even really like scrapbooking, and this meeting had the potential to become embarrassing, especially if he were the only guy there. But he liked thinking about colour schemes and design elements, so at least it might not be a total bore, and if he got to sit next to Trinity, then that was a bonus. "I'd love to come, if the meeting really is today."

Trinity smiled. She was wearing this dark red-purple lipstick that made her teeth look snow-white, and lent a warm glow to her cool, porcelain skin. "I'd like that."

It turned out that the meeting wasn't that day, it was tomorrow, like Ellie had said. So Zack ate lunch with them instead of his other friends. Zack tried to pay attention to both Trinity and Ellie—but it was so hard. It wasn't that Ellie wasn't attractive. Zack didn't have anything against blondes, and judging by the muscles peeking out from her sleeve, Ellie hit the gym often enough. But Trinity...she had this glow about her. She got him, even on that first day.

When the bell rang, neither Trinity nor Zack moved from their seats. They had spent the entire lunch hour in the cafeteria. Ellie stood and stretched; Zack watched as she bent backwards until her back cracked. Letting out a satisfied sigh, she gathered her garbage and balled it in her hands. "We'd better get to Chemistry, Trin."

"Oh...yeah." She stood slowly, grabbing at the empty paper plate that was covered in dried grease from her pizza slice, keeping her gaze fixed on him. "What do you have next?"

"Art class," he replied. "In the computer lab."

"Oh." It was a disappointed "oh." The computer lab was in a different wing than the chemistry lab.

"You wanna do something tonight?" Zack found himself asking. He hadn't meant to ask her in front of Ellie, but she was on her way to the garbage can. Whether she did that purposely to give them a private moment, Zack didn't know, but it was something else that he was extremely grateful for.

A smile spread across Trinity's face. "I like Thai food."

"Me too."

They exchanged cell phone numbers before Ellie whisked Trinity away to her chemistry class. Zack took his time gathering his things and whistled a tune as he made his way to the computer lab.

Their first date was really nothing out of the ordinary. They went to a little Thai place off Spring Garden Road and shared some spring rolls and jasmine tea. Zack ordered the Pad Thai while Trinity ordered the Ginger Chicken. Neither of them had to look at the menu for long to know what they wanted, for which Zack was glad; the menu hid his view of Trinity's glowing face.

And the smiling. It seemed to Zack that he could've just leaned across the table and kissed her right there, in front of the other twenty-or-so people in the restaurant, and that would've been okay, but instead he kept his chopsticks in hand and asked her about scrapbooking.

"I don't know why I do it, really. It's expensive and my mom thinks I should spend more time on a more useful extracircular, like sports or something." She shrugged and gracefully picked up a sticky glob of rice with her chopsticks.

"Well, if you like it, you should do it."

"Yeah." Her smile returned, slowly. "What do you want to do?"

Kiss you, he thought. "Right now?"

"With your life."

Zack shrugged. "A graphic designer, probably. Gotta build my portfolio first though. You?"

Her eyes lit up as she set her chopsticks on her napkin. "I have a plan."

"Oh yeah?"

"Yeah. You wanna hear it?"

"Sure."

"Okay. So I'm taking French Immersion right now, and I'm doing a Spanish class next semester, so I was thinking that as long as I can maintain my A average, I'll apply to Dalhousie, and become a translator."

"A translator. Really?"

"Yeah. *Nihongo wo hanashimasu ka?*"

Zack chuckled. "I only speak a little bit. I understand more than I can speak."

"What can you say. Teach me something." Her breasts pressed against the table as she leaned forward, and he had to be careful not to let his gaze linger on them.

"*Anata wa utsukushii,*" he said quietly. *You are beautiful.*

"What does that mean?" she asked.

He bit his lip and shook his head. "Guess."

This time Trinity laughed, her smile brighter than the lanterns hanging from the ceiling. "Could mean anything!"

"But it doesn't. Guess."

She leaned back in her chair, took her mango juice in hand,

and studied him thoughtfully. "Does it mean...'I like peanut sauce?'"

"Nope."

"How about...'I like your shirt'." She pulled playfully at the frills above just below her right shoulder.

"Why do you think it means that I like something?"

"I don't know." She seemed a little disappointed at that, but he could see her trying to calculate a way around it. He knew she knew it meant something flirty—the game wouldn't be fun otherwise—but whether or not she would rise to the occasion, Zack didn't know.

"Is it something I can say to you?" she asked.

Now it was Zack's turn to blush. "If you want to, I guess."

"So it is a compliment, then."

"Maybe."

She didn't say anything for a few minutes as she picked up her chopsticks and resumed eating, but her face retained a warm glow for the rest of the evening.

"So," Zack said, changing the subject slightly. "Was that the end of Trinity Hartell's grand plan? Go to Dalhousie and become a translator?"

"No," she replied. "I'm going to travel, maybe live in Germany or Switzerland for a while, and learn German there. I'd like to know at least four languages minimum, but ideally seven. English and French, of course, Spanish, German, Japanese, Mandarin and Finnish. Finnish just sounds like...it's so beautiful. If elves existed, like Lord of the Rings elves, Finnish would be their language." She talked with her hands, and Zack couldn't help being caught up in her excitement, so much so that he barely heard her when she added, "so what's the word beautiful in Japanese?"

Zack opened his mouth to tell her, but then thought better of it. She crossed her arms in silent victory as he signalled to the waiter as he walked past. "We'll have the bill now."

By the time they left the restaurant, it was dark and the few stars you can see in Halifax were out, twinkling away with the city lights. It was a chilly September night and although there weren't many people around, you never knew when someone was going to jump out. Zack extended his arm and Trinity wrapped herself around it, giving his muscles a subtle squeeze.

"You work out!" she exclaimed.

It was quite a long walk from Spring Garden Road back to the Quinpool Road, but the time passed too quickly as they strolled, sometimes in silence, sometimes talking about school and their dreams. Although the climb was difficult, they walked around the base of Citadel Hill—on the other side of the road, of course, just in case the rumours about there being prostitutes and johns on the hill were true.

When they came to the Commons, Trinity urged him to stop. "Let's go around."

Zack scanned the grounds. Trinity was right to be cautious. Some scary shit could go down there—even though it was an open field, and near their high school, it was a notorious location for drug deals and sometimes you could be mugged by groups of young men. It looked empty, but Zack didn't want to chance ruining their perfect date—and he would take any opportunity to prolong its end.

So they continued along Bell Road until it turned into Quinpool, and turned up to Windsor towards Duncan Street. Trinity's arm slipped from his but her fingers hovered around his hand; an invitation that Zack accepted. Her fingers were slightly cold from the early fall air. He squeezed warmth into them, and she squeezed back.

"Well...this is me," she said as they stopped in front of a white-yellow house with large front windows and stairs leading up to the front door. Two stained glass hangings hung daintily inside, one of some kind of flower and the other a large golden "H", presumably for Hartell.

For a moment neither of them spoke, and Zack looked at his feet. He knew what he was supposed to do, but if she rejected him…

"*Anata wa utsukushii*…it means that I think you're beautiful," he said finally.

She lifted her head, her eyes twinkling. "I know."

"You do?"

"Yeah…I just wanted to hear you say it in English."

And then, possessed by a fit of courage and lust and the butterflies of first love, Zack bent to kiss her. Her lips were soft and tasted like watermelon lip chap, layered with the spiciness of their meal. When their lips parted, they were wearing matching smiles. He cupped her face gently and preserved the moment—the light reflecting in her eyes, the smell of her lilac perfume and the peanut sauce lingering on both their breaths—and he said, "Be my girlfriend?"

She balanced herself on her tiptoes and pressed her forehead against his. "I'm yours."

*

Zack snapped awake. For a moment, he forgot where he was—the foreign smells of the hospital, plastic and sick people and annoyed people waiting their turns—made him want to puke. Cold shivers went down his spine as he searched the walls for a clock. How long had he been sleeping? He jumped to his feet and steadied himself—sleep was still near. Had he missed the doctor? Was Trinity…?

No, Trinity's parents were right where he'd left them. Stephanie, pacing back and forth in front of the wall by the receptionist's desk, absently running her fingers through the back of the straw-coloured hair that fell messily around her shoulders. George fiddled with his iPhone as he leaned against the wall; his slouching made Stephanie look taller than she already was. It looked like he hadn't shaved in days and that, combined with the upset of his usually well-groomed moustache, made him look homeless.

Stephanie looked at Zack with sad eyes as he shuffled towards her. "Have you been here…?"

"…same as you guys, yeah," Zack finished.

Stephanie's mascara stained her cheeks and whatever eye shadow she'd been wearing was on the back of her hands. "You have school tomorrow. You should—"

"And you have work. Are you going to that?"

"One of us is going to have to go," she said, mostly to George.

George pocketed his phone and wrapped an arm around his wife. "We can both stay. Phone Mr. Dalton—"

"We don't know when she's going to wake up, or if—"

"Stephanie—"

"We have to be realistic—"

"She will—!"

Their argument cooled and then hushed to silence as a man in a white lab coat came out of Trinity's hospital room. Zack braced himself on the wall and prepared himself for the worst. He had to be strong. Trinity would like that.

"How is she?" Stephanie asked the doctor, whose nametag said "LETOFSKY." Her fingers intertwined with her husband's as if they were praying.

"She's stabilized," Dr. Letofsky replied. "You can see her now."

"Is she conscious?" Zack asked.

It didn't even feel like he spoke. It was like some other Zack had spoken through him, some other Zack that was paying more attention to the goings on of the hospital, the Zack that was living in the here and now and not stuck in Ellie's 2010 Toyota with visions of blood-spattered, skull-crushed Trinity.

"She's in a coma," Dr. Letofsky said slowly.

Coma. Coma meant alive. Not dead. A flicker of hope flared inside Zack like a lighter trying to shine brightly in the rain.

"Will...will she wake up?" he asked.

Dr. Letofsky twisted his lips and shrugged. "We're not sure."

Stephanie let out a sob, and then hurried for Trinity's room. George followed. Zack wondered if he should hang back—if it was more important for Trinity's parents to see her first—but realized it was his own fear of seeing Trinity vulnerable that paralyzed his feet and glued them to the hospital tiles.

He dragged himself in the room with his eyes wide open so that he would not shy away from whatever crippled form he had imagined her to be. His imagination had greatly exaggerated. She looked as if she were sleeping, peaceful, were it not for the bruises and scrapes that marred her face. Her forehead was wrapped in white gauze; she had had some sort of operation—oh God, on her brain, was it?—but as Trinity's parents inspected her daughter, he couldn't help but feel a sense of relief. She was breathing—the blankets were disturbed by her slow breaths. That was the most important thing to him in that moment. Even if she never did wake up (no, he couldn't think about that possibility) at least she was alive, and he could be with her. He vowed not to leave her side until she awoke.

Hours—maybe days—passed.

It was just Zack and Stephanie by Trinity's side. George had gone home to cook supper, as none of them had had a proper meal in at least two days. The hospital room became Zack's entire existence. It was so easy to forget that the world continued without them. Although Zack hadn't been on the internet since the accident, Stephanie mentioned during a moment of small talk that someone had created a Facebook group called, "Praying for Trinity."

Praying. Was that all they could do? Was that all that could be done? Where were the scientists and the medical miracles in the world when they were most needed? There's a good chance she won't wake up, they said instead. Even if she does, she might not be the same—she might not walk, or talk, or like the same things. There's not much we can do, Zack, except pray.

Trinity—the only girl he ever dared to say the L word to—lay helpless, and all people could do was turn to fucking God?

If He even existed. Stephanie seemed to think He existed. She sat across from Zack, gripping her silver cross necklace so tight that her knuckles turned white and imprinted Christ's sorry state onto her palm. Her other hand gripped Trinity's, which was impaled with tubes and plastic things that were supposed to be keeping her alive.

Zack gripped Trinity's other hand. Her left eye was blackened, and there were tons of little cuts and bruises from where she had hit the pavement. She was lucky to not have broken any bones; at least, no one told him that she had broken any bones. Her head and chin were wrapped in white gauze. Throw on the black headdress and she would've looked like a nun.

But no, if Zack had to compare her to anything, it had to be an angel. And if there was really a God out there, he quietly prayed that He let this angel wake up, at least one last time, to let him know that she was still alive.

"You've been here for hours, Zack," Stephanie said, her voice gravelly from not talking for a while. "You don't have to stay."

He shook his head. "It's all right. I want to."

"I'm…I'm sure she appreciates it."

Zack reached out with his free hand and caressed the non-bruised, non-cut parts of Trinity's cheek. If God could give him the power of Photoshop, he'd erase all of her blemishes, and then paint them on the fucking bastard that rammed his truck into their lives and created this chaos.

"Do you have any homework that needs to be brought over to you?" Stephanie asked.

"No I…" Homework. That was something he'd have to think about later. His teachers would understand, right? They had to. Trinity was more important than grades anyway. "I'll do it later."

Stephanie smiled, but it didn't quite reach her tear-stained eyes.

"Have you slept yet?" Zack asked.

"Um, no. I'm fine." She nodded several times, as if that made it true, and wrapped the necklace chain around her fingers and squeezed.

"You look like you could use some coffee."

Stephanie glanced at Trinity, and then to the door. "Maybe…"

"I can go get it for you, if you want."

"No, that's fine, Zack. I'll get some." Stephanie carefully pried her fingers from Trinity and stood. She padded her purple flowery skirt down with the hand that held the cross and put on a false smile that was supposed to make them both feel better. "You stay with Trinity. Want anything?"

"No…no thanks. I'm good."

Stephanie squeezed Zack's shoulder on the way out, and he realized how tense his muscles were. The door opened and closed softly behind him.

Zack didn't notice the change immediately. The machine that monitored Trinity's vitals started beeping faster, and more regularly.

Then, her eyes flickered open.

"Holy shit! Trin. Trinity!" He looked to the door and waved his hand like a mad man, hoping some nurse or Dr. Letofsky would walk by. "Someone get in here, quick! She's awake!"

Trinity murmured something inaudible. A few tears escaped Zack's eyes and dripped onto the off-white hospital bed sheets.

"It's me, Zack," he said, his voice cracking. "You remember me, right?"

Her eyes slid lazily to his and stared, as if they were trying to search for something that she couldn't quite grasp. Then they moved to Zack's hand, intertwined with hers. She pulled away quickly.

"Why...you...sad?" she asked.

Her speech was slow and careful, and she pronounced each word like it was her first. But Zack didn't care.

"You can talk! Thank God!" Wait, thank God? Oh who cared. She was alive, damn it! "They told me you wouldn't be able to talk anymore."

More tears followed. He reached for her hand, but it was out of his grasp. He wiped the tears on his jacket and sniffled. She watched him intently, like a frightened animal.

"Why are you crying?" she asked.

"Trin...don't you remember?" Zack sniffled. "The accident?" He pronounced the word like it was secret, or taboo.

He noticed that Trinity tried to match his weeping facial expression. "Ax...uh...dent?"

"Yeah, Trin. Don't you remember? You were in the car...and then...you weren't...?"

She stared at him blankly.

"Oh, well they said you might not remember," Zack said, wiping the rest of the tears away with the back of his hand. "I don't know whether I should tell you or not."

Trinity, squeezing his hand as she reached for her cell phone. Trinity, flying out the back windshield. Glass, everywhere. Blood, everywhere. Rain, washing it all away.

"You...you were in the car with me and Ellie. And then this jerkoff came out of nowhere..."

Trinity touched her bandaged head, and frowned. "I...hurt me?"

Zack nodded. "Yeah."

"You cry...'cause I hurt?"

"Oh Trin..."

"Who are you?"

The question came out of nowhere, like being punched in the nuts, and the shock spread throughout his body. "What?"

"Who are you?" she repeated.

"Trin, what do you mean?" He paused. "It's me, Zack. Your boyfriend."

She looked at him as if he were speaking a foreign language. Zack leapt to his feet in frustration.

"How could you not remember? One year, seven months, Trin! That's how long we've been together. I never kept track, but you always reminded me. Please tell me you remember some of it...please, Trinity, please..."

He fell to his knees beside the hospital bed and looked up at her, pleading, clutching the bed sheets. She stared at him with child-like fascination.

"We...we were going to go to Dal together. You'd just gotten your acceptance letter, a day before mine. We...we were thinking about an apartment."

"You're sad again," was all she said.

He didn't want to cry again. His lips trembled as he buried them in the bed sheets, smelling the faint scent of Tide and baby wipes as he sobbed for Trinity's lost memories, her death. He felt a light tugging sensation on his dark brown strands of hair—she was playing with them, twirling them in her fingers and humming to herself.

The door opened behind him. Zack heard a mug crash on the tiles as Stephanie ran to Trinity's side.

"Trinity...my baby! You're awake..."

"Mommy!" Trinity squealed.

She stopped playing with Zack's hair and embraced her mother as if she hadn't seen her in years.

"Mommy…bad dream," Trinity said. "Then…woke up, and I…here, and…man sad…who?"

Stephanie's eyes darted between her daughter and Zack, mirroring his initial shock. She reached across the hospital bed and took Zack's hand in hers, and squeezed.

*

Dr. Letofsky slapped a CT scan of Trinity's brain on the clipboard in his office.

"The trauma was likely caused by both the acceleration when she was thrown from the car, and when she hit the pavement," Dr. Letofsky explained. "She's taken heavy damage to her parietal lobe, frontal lobe and temporal lobe, but her language functions are pretty much intact."

Stephanie and George sat in the two comfy chairs in front of Dr. Letofsky's desk, while Zack leaned against the open doorway. He smelled like stale sweat and he'd only changed his clothes once since he'd gotten to the hospital, and that was only when his parents wagged a washed shirt and pair of jeans in front of him, insisting that it would be good for Trinity's health for him to change. He wasn't sure if he should be in the office or watching Trinity, but she seemed content to play in the waiting room.

Zack glanced into the waiting room. Trinity's physical recovery in the last week was the only miracle he'd seen so far. She still wore bandages around her head and chest, but she was allowed to walk around with assistance. Now, she sat on the floor, gripping a Barbie by its waist. A toy convertible with two other Barbies—a Ken and a Skipper—was parked next to Trinity's knees. The Barbie she held hopped up and down on the front windshield, causing the convertible to rock. The Ken fell over in his seat.

Stephanie studied the CT scan of Trinity's brain. "What does that mean, doctor?"

Dr. Letofsky looked grim. He intertwined his fingers as his eyes went from George, and then to Stephanie. "Not enough time has passed to diagnose her with anything concrete, but I do want to prepare you for the potential behavioural changes she may experience."

"Like what?" George asked.

The doctor softened his voice. "People with this kind of brain damage often have difficulty connecting with others. That is usually the most stressful change that families have to learn to cope with. Trinity may have lost a significant portion of her memories, which adds to this stress."

That was the worst part, Zack wanted to say.

"Another symptom that is quite common is a preoccupation with certain objects or subjects—she may spend hours doing one activity. She will probably be much more inflexible and angrier than normal, especially if you try to stop her from continuing an obsessive behaviour. She will also most likely have reduced reading and writing skills—possibly down to a lower elementary level."

The news was like a dark smoke cloud that hovered above their heads. Stephanie took a deep breath, and for a moment Zack thought she might cry again, but instead she seemed to suck all of her sadness inside her and hid it behind a mask of little emotion. "But that doesn't mean that Trinity will be that that. Right?"

"I'd rather prepare you for the worst-case scenario, Ms. Hartell," Dr. Letofsky replied. "In truth, there's little else we can do for Trinity here. If she returns to a familiar environment she may be able to recover some of her lost skills and memories."

Zack felt a flicker of hope inside him. "Will she ever be normal again?"

The three adults turned to look at him, as if realizing for the first time that he was in the room.

"The varying definition of normal aside...the long and short of it is that we don't know," Dr. Letofsky replied. "If given the proper stimulation, a familiar environment...it could be possible that her memories will return. Whether or not she will behave as other teens her age do, or even as she did before, it's difficult to say."

"So, she should go back to school," Zack said.

"That would be up to Ms. and Mr. Hartell."

Stephanie and George exchanged glances, and for a moment, neither of them spoke.

"We'll have to talk about that," George said finally.

"Citadel High does have special needs programs," Stephanie pointed out.

"Yes, but having her go back to school so soon? With strange teachers?"

"George, if she stays home, one or both of us have to stay home with her. And I can't...you know I can't, not at this crucial stage..."

"I can come look after her," Zack offered, stepping forward.

George patted him on the arm. "That's...that's very kind of you, Zack, but I don't think your parents would let you—"

"I don't care."

"His parents have let him stay here all week. Maybe it isn't..." Stephanie started to say, but she trailed off after George gave her a "are you crazy" look.

"I can recommend you some psychiatrists that specialize in mentally challenged teenagers," Dr. Letofsky said, digging through his papers to produce a notepad and a pen.

Mentally Challenged. It was a horrifying label that Zack couldn't bear to place on Trinity. She was just sick, that's all. A bump on the head. She just needed to go back to school with him and remember who she really was.

"I'm going to give you the number of a psychiatrist as well, Zack. It might be good to talk to someone who isn't your parents about this," the doctor said, tearing off a slip of paper. He scribbled something on it and then held it out for Zack to take.

Zack didn't want to see a shrink. He was the one that was fine. He just wanted Trinity to get better, to be normal again. But Stephanie craned her neck to look at him again with that false encouraging smile, the "yes, go ahead and be a good boy" smile. He tried to return it but his face felt sour as he took the psychiatrist's number from Dr. Letofsky.

The adults continued talking about other things but their voices became distant echoes compared to his swirling emotions. The doctor was wrong. Trinity wasn't going to receive the care she needed from any shrink. She was supposed to go to university with him. He was going to take care of her, to protect her from all the bad things that would hurt her. He promised that he would not leave her. When she saw his unwavering commitment to her, she'd remember him.

She had to.

CHAPTER THREE

Ellie had taken gymnastics mostly to get away from her parents. They had divorced when she was in junior high and the bitterness of the end of their relationship hung in their house like the smell of stale sweat in a locker room. Her father got to keep their house in downtown Halifax, so her mom moved out to Lawrencetown—which was about forty-five minutes away. Since Ellie didn't want to switch schools, it was arranged so that she would spend her weekdays with her father, and the weekends with her mother.

Even though her dad travelled a lot on business and left her to her own devices, the house was often cold. Her mother had taken most of the furniture, leaving a shell of her childhood home behind. When her father was around, he tried to pretend like nothing major had changed. When her mother came to pick her up, she was cold and distant until they were across the Macdonald or the MacKay bridge, as if having a mass of salt water between her and her former husband put her mind at ease.

The gymnastics class was three times a week: Monday, Wednesday and Friday after school. At first, her muscles burned and cried with each movement after class, but as the classes went on, she found herself looking forward to each lesson, and she felt her body grow stronger every day. Where the other girls started developing breasts, she developed toned arms and legs.

There was one Friday where Trinity had offered to drive Ellie back to her mother's place after gymnastics, since Trinity had an after-school Spanish lesson.

They were nearing the car, which was parked on the street beside the school when she showed Trinity the paper. "Look at this."

Trinity took the paper gingerly from Ellie's hands and studied it. "Gymnastics competition? Here?"

"Yeah!" Ellie skipped the rest of the way to the car and would've done a back flip if it weren't for the asphalt, and the traffic zipping by them. "It's kind of expensive but my parents will cover it. They have to!"

"Why wouldn't they?" Trinity asked as she unlocked the car.

Ellie bit her lip. It was hard to explain to Trinity sometimes that she had it good when it came to parents. It had been a few years since Ellie's parents had split, and since then, finances had been tight. If Ellie wasn't working so hard in school and in gymnastics, she was sure that they would have made her get a part-time job somewhere.

"They will," Ellie said again, to convince herself.

After making a quick stop at the bank so that Trinity could get some cash, Trinity drove them both to Ellie's mother's house. They found Ms. Beverly Emerson in the kitchen, still in her nightdress, with the newspaper in one hand and a highlighter in the other. The cordless phone stood at attention beside her. Since the divorce she'd been forced to leave her job and she was trying to find similar work in Dartmouth. Judging from her dress, Ellie supposed she hadn't had any interviews today.

"Hi Mom," Ellie said, dropping her bookbag by the pantry. "Trinity's here."

Beverly's hazel eyes flickered up to greet them, and Ellie noted that at least she had put on some makeup. "Trinity, honey. Thank you for driving Ellie."

"You're welcome," Trinity said.

"Anything you'd like, you can get it yourself," Beverly said in a sickly sweet voice that made Ellie cringe.

"I'm fine, thank you," Trinity replied shyly, tucking a strand of hair around her ear.

Beverly's smile was thin as she returned to her newspaper. "How was school today?"

"Mom, there's a gymnastics competition in a couple of weeks," Ellie blurted out. She brought the information over to her mother as she put aside her highlighter and newspaper. "It's really important to me that I compete."

"Is there prize money if you win?" Beverly asked.

"There's a trophy," Ellie said. "Can I go Mom, please?"

Ms. Emerson took one fleeting look at the paper and slid it across the table. "The registration fee is sixty-five dollars."

"So?"

Sighing, she shook her head. "I can't do that this month. Your dentist appointment was only last week and I had to cover that myself. Maybe your father will pay for it."

"But Dad won't be back for another three weeks!"

Trinity was examining the fridge magnets, probably pretending she couldn't hear. Ellie hoped she was doing more than pretending. You'd think she'd at least leave the room...no, this wasn't Trinity's fault, she couldn't take it out on her. It was her parents, her dumb parents who could never get along and always fought for the stupidest reasons.

"Well, then you have your answer." She reached into her pocket and pulled out her pack of cigarettes.

Ellie slumped in her chair, her cheeks reddening. "Don't do that in here. It's disgusting."

"Trinity, honey, you don't mind if I light up in here, do you?"

Trinity turned and put on a polite smile, but Ellie could see the look of disapproval in her eyes. "I…don't mind."

"See? Trinity doesn't mind, so why should you?"

Ellie pushed back the chair and shoved it back into the table with a thundering crack that almost split the wood. "Fine. Your lungs can rot. See if I care."

"Ellie Emerson! Is that any way to treat your mother?"

She ignored her as she grabbed Trinity's arm and pulled her down the stairs. "Let's get out of here," she whispered.

"I want an apology!" her mother called after her.

Ellie's room was the first on the left, and as soon as she and Trinity were in, she shut the door to muffle her mother's cries, and hopefully to dull the cigarette smoke.

"I'm…sorry."

She spun around. Trinity hovered near the door like she wanted to escape. Ellie felt bad for exposing her to her mother. This was why they always went to Trinity's house. Now she would feel bad for her, and Ellie couldn't stand it when people pitied her.

"Your mom. I shouldn't have encouraged her," Trinity continued.

Ellie scoffed and belly-flopped on to her bed. "You were just being polite. It's not like you can say no to her in her own house."

Trinity sat on the edge of the bed and scooped up her purse. Ellie leaned back on her pillows and stared at her digital clock. Quarter after four. Still time to get out of here and find their own supper, maybe McDonald's or something closer.

She was about to suggest this when Trinity placed something on Ellie's chest. It was a bundle of tens and fives, neatly folded in half. "Here."

Ellie sat up and the money tumbled into her lap. "What's this for?"

"You want to compete, right?"

"Yeah....?"

"So take it."

At first, she was too stunned to speak. Her best friend was going to give her money because she was too poor to pay the entry fee. It was something out of a horrible novel or movie where the underdog rose up and defeated whatever challenged her. Ellie did not want to be that challenged person—she just wanted to win.

"Where did you get all of this money?"

Trinity shrugged. "Savings. I was going to buy a new dress for the Spring Formal, but I'm sure I've got something in my closet I can wear."

The answer only made Ellie angry, and more embarrassed than ever. Trinity had more money than her. She could take it out of her bank account to buy nice things. Her mother and father were in control of her bank account, and besides, if she took anything out she was afraid she wouldn't be able to have enough for university. Goddamnit, to take charity from Trinity?

"I can't," Ellie said, leafing through the bills. "It's too much."

"No, it isn't." Trinity squeezed Ellie's hands together, as if to glue them to the money. "I'm your friend and I want you to be happy."

"But—"

"No, I don't want it back." Trinity leapt off the bed and backed away to the other side of the room.

Ellie looked down at the bills again. "I'll pay you back, I promise."

"Nope."

"No?"

Trinity folded her arms. "Consider it a Christmas present and a birthday present all rolled into one."

"Trin..."

"You're going to pay the fee and then you're going to win. Right?"

Placing the money on top of her digital clock, Ellie managed a smile. "Well..."

"Yes, you will!" Trinity insisted. "You're going to be in the competition."

Looking back, Ellie knew she should have hugged her in that moment. But how could she have known what would happen? Instead she savoured the feeling of Trinity's confidence in her and wrapped that around her heart, hoping it would soothe any previous wounds from her poor self-esteem.

*

The second-place metal that hung around her bedpost, jingling slightly as Ellie leapt off her bed to answer the phone, caused her to remember that moment. She glanced at the place where Trinity had stood defiant, generous, proud. So sure of a happy ending.

Zack's cell phone number showed up on the caller ID. Ellie's stomach fluttered as she grabbed the receiver, shut the door and crawled into bed. "Hello."

"Hi, Ellie," Zack said.

There was a note of sadness in his voice that made Ellie's throat tighten. "What...what happened? Is everything all right? Is she...?"

"She's awake."

Ellie leaned back into her pillows and breathed a sigh of relief as Zack filled her in on the details. The phone was so tightly pressed against her ear that it began to ache, but she didn't care. Trinity didn't die. Ellie didn't kill her. It was like someone had lifted a weight from her shoulders and chest, and she could breathe again.

"Thank God she's alive," she said after he was done.

The door of her bedroom creaked open. Her mom was carrying a laundry basket filled with Ellie's clean clothes. "Who are you talking to?"

"It's Zack," Ellie replied quickly.

"Is Trinity all right?"

That was probably the first time her mom had asked that question, Ellie realized. Her mom had freaked when she heard what had happened to the car. She didn't know all the details about the insurance, but apparently when they traced the license plate number of the truck that hit them, it turned out to be registered to a fake company. That obviously raised some police eyebrows but mostly, for Ellie's mom, it meant that the insurance company might not replace the car. Which really, really sucked. Her dad and her mom fought about it a lot, and Ellie worried that what little her parents had saved for Ellie to go to university might go to replacing the car.

"Ellie? Are you still there?" Zack asked.

She threw the blankets over her head and switched the phone to her other ear. "I'm here. It's just my mom."

"Your supper is cold downstairs. If you want it, you'll have to heat it up." And then her mother shut the door, leaving her alone with Zack—even if he was in the city and she was stuck in Lawerencetown.

"So, yeah," he said. He sighed, creating static on the phone. "How have you been doing?"

"I'm supposed to see a counsellor tomorrow."

"Me too, I think. It's bullshit. I want to be here, with Trin. My 'rents might make me go back to school though, now that Trinity is awake and all."

"I got all your homework for you." Ellie peeked out of the blankets and eyed the stack of papers on her desk. She had used two of her lunch hours to track down all of Zack's teachers and get all of the assignments. That Zack would soon return to school—it was a hope she could cling to that wasn't tempered by the uncertainty of Trinity's coma.

"Ellie…you didn't have to do that."

"I wanted to," she blurted out, and then smacked herself. No, no, she had to be careful about that. She quickly regained control. "When exactly are you coming back to school?"

"Might not be 'til next week. I don't really feel like…well, you know. Still gotta do counselling, but it's not going to be through the school."

Ellie was envious of that. Neither her mother nor her father could afford to give her to a real psychologist, one that wasn't funded by the school. And she couldn't afford to miss any school or assignments herself, not if she wanted to keep up her attendance and good grades. Scholarships were going to be a big factor in what university she would attend.

"Would you mind…uh…getting my assignments and stuff until then?" he asked.

"Of course I will. And I could find a way to get them to you."

Yes, she could imagine it now. She'd drop off the assignments to Zack after school, and then they'd get a chance to hang out…

"Well, I'm leaving tomorrow to go visit my aunt…I think my parents want to get me away from the hospital. Part of me doesn't blame them. Seeing her look at me like that…I mean, she doesn't even know me," He was trying to make it into a joke, she could hear his forced smile. "Maybe she'll know you. Who knows."

"Yeah." Ellie felt like there was a fire in her stomach. She curled into the foetal position and wished she could take him into her arms and make everything better. "I'm sorry, Zack."

"It wasn't your fault, Ellie. You have nothing to be sorry for."

"I just…" She couldn't say it. Now was not the time. "Everything's going to be different now."

Her words seemed to sit with Zack a while, and Ellie watched her digital clock as she listened to him breathe over the phone, never wanting to hang up. Never wanting to let go.

"I should let you get to sleep. It's getting late," he said finally.

"I'm not tired," she replied. "But…but yeah."

"My mom will come to the school tomorrow to get the assignments, okay?"

"Okay. I'll….save the rest for you when you get back."

"Thanks Ellie. You're…you're the best."

She broke out into a giant grin. That compliment would keep her up half the night daydreaming. "You're my friend, Zack. I'd do anything for you."

"Yeah…well, I really appreciate this."

"It's no problem, really." Anything for his praise.

"I'll talk to you later, okay?"

"Okay."

"Have a good night."

"Sleep well," she said, but the receiver clicked, and he was already gone.

Chapter Four

Trinity was deemed well enough to come home two weeks later. Most of her wounds had healed, but the scar where her head had hit the pavement would stay there for the rest of her life.

George was able to get a few days off work to look after Trinity, but he couldn't take an extended leave. He was needed at the office. So it fell upon Stephanie to ask for a leave of absence from her job—something that pained her greatly.

Stephanie drove quietly from their home on Duncan Street and turned onto Quinpool. The campaign signs were springing up on the lawns more often now. Wiley Dalton's smiling face was plastered on most of them, thanks to Stephanie's efforts. It was the one thing that was holding her together, besides the dangling silver cross that wrapped around the rear-view mirror. She had hoped to see the entire campaign through after spending hours on fundraisers, arranging public speaking arrangements, and kissing babies.

Wiley would understand, she told herself. He wasn't one of those false politicians that said one thing and did another. When she talked, he actually listened, staring at her with those intense green eyes of his, and his laugh boomed like he was connected to an amplifier. She had helped to make him, and if he didn't win this year's mayoral election, goddamnit, what else did she have in this world?

George didn't understand this. He was her husband of almost twenty years and she loved him dearly, but she was sure he had never done anything that made him feel as alive as she did when she was campaigning for Wiley. George had pleaded with her last night while they lay in bed together: "I'm a vice president at an information technology company and I haven't got much vacation time. You're a volunteer campaign organizer. We can afford to have you not work for a little while, at least until we figure out what Trinity's long term care plan is going to be."

"I thought we had this figured out. The school has special programs—"

"She's not in school all day! I don't get home until after six, and sometimes you're not home until later than that."

"So we'll hire a babysitter."

The look he gave her—it was like she had just stabbed him in the chest. It was so painful that she felt like she had been stabbed too. A babysitter. Well, she wasn't exactly acting like a teenager anymore. Leaning across her night table, she turned off the light so that she wouldn't have to see his face. While she lay there, pretending not to care about her seeming not to care, George said nothing. She went to sleep while he remained propped up against the baseboard.

The next morning had been tense. Stephanie could barely see the surface of the dining room table; it was covered old and new schedules she'd made for Wiley. George took his breakfast in front of the TV while Stephanie munched on a piece of unbuttered toast and organized her papers. Trinity was with him; she could hear her screeching and laughing like a toddler. Which she was now, Stephanie supposed.

Wasn't that every mother's dream, to see their children as adorable babies again? Stephanie peeked into the living room. Trinity was wearing a mismatched stripped tank top and a flowery skirt—Stephanie didn't have the time or patience to put her in pants, and Trinity seemed to be happier that way. She was staring mindlessly at the TV, her mouth occasionally twitching when something mildly funny was said. It was hard to see her as a seventeen-year-old girl anymore. The way she sat, her legs splayed open, so that you could see her frilly blue underwear. Saliva occasionally dripped from her open mouth—one of the minor physical side effects of the brain damage; she sometimes "forgot" to swallow. When Stephanie walked into the room, George ignored her, but Trinity's attention wavered.

"Mommy," she said, with a nod to confirm Stephanie's identity.

"George." Stephanie cleared her throat, but he still wouldn't look at her. Fine. She knew he could hear her. "I'll ask him for a leave of absence."

"And if he doesn't give it to you?" George took a big bite of his peanut butter toast sandwich—some of the peanut butter got in his moustache.

Stephanie sucked air through her teeth. "Then maybe I'll quit."

George grunted. "Maybe?"

"I'm asking. Isn't that enough?" She stormed out of the room, grabbed her briefcase and flew down the hallway to the front door.

"Stephanie…"

He was just behind her, reaching for her, but she slammed the door before he could say anything else. After manoeuvring the morning traffic for another fifteen minutes, she finally arrived at the Barrington Street campaign office. She parked in the lot, and retrieved her black briefcase from the trunk. Goosebumps appeared on her arms, and it wasn't from the chill winds that blew up from the harbour. She slammed the trunk and took a deep breath. She could do this. He would understand. No one knew him better than she did. But whether or not he would say yes…

Because there was a large part of her that hoped he said no. And if he did say no…maybe she could convince George that a full-time specialist caretaker was a good idea. Maybe Wiley would give her a raise instead to help pay for that…yes. Yes, this was a good plan. Ask for the unreasonable thing first, and then the more reasonable thing…that was her university psychology knowledge at work.

Like a proud bird displaying its feathers, Stephanie entered the campaign office. It wasn't anything special. There were a couple desks pushed up against the walls with Staples office chairs. Young women and men—all volunteers—sat at them, talking on the phone, spreading Wiley's influence to the Haligonians. They looked up at her as she passed—some of the older ones had obviously heard the news about Trinity. She nodded in curt greeting but didn't let any emotion slip through. If she showed weakness, they would fail, and all would be lost. They would need every vote to win. Posters of Wiley adorned the walls, encouraging everyone to VOTE FOR EXPERIENCE AND A BETTER TOMORROW.

The headquarters consisted of one front room, and two private offices in the back—one for Wiley, and one for Stephanie. Wiley's had a window that looked into the front room. The shades were drawn, but the lights were on. He was probably enjoying his morning Tim Horton's, feet propped up on his paperless desk, surfing the web for the next community event that he could drop by.

She didn't bother to knock. She opened the door and immediately froze. Wiley was pacing behind his desk, speaking in hushed tones into his cell phone.

"I told you, we don't want him! Get someone else!" Pause. Muffled male voice on the other end chattering non-stop. Wiley interrupted him. "Fine, fine! But next time, tell me before grabbing one that big. We don't have the space or the time—"

Stephanie cleared her throat. Wiley looked up at her. His wide shoulders gave him an intimidating manner of a football player, but only to those who didn't know him; she felt safe and protected in his presence.

"I'll call you back," he said, and flipped the cell shut.

"Was I interrupting something important?" Stephanie asked as she shut the door.

Wiley flashed her a smile. His teeth were perfectly straight—he had had braces when he was younger, she was sure—and artificially whitened. "Not really. My daughter's getting married, and well, it's a whole mess, really. Chaos."

Stephanie raised an eyebrow. "I didn't know you had a daughter."

"She's out west, with her mother. I haven't seen her in about five years, since I moved here."

She sensed a difficult topic and steered the conversation elsewhere. It was already hard enough to bring up her own daughter. She placed her briefcase on the chair in front of her and ran her hands through her hair, making sure there were no flyaways.

"Hey, listen." He walked towards her and placed a gentle hand on her shoulder. His eyes were a deep shade of green that reminded Stephanie of a peaceful meadow. "I heard what happened. I didn't know if you were coming in today, but I left some flowers on your desk."

Stephanie blushed. "Flowers! You really didn't have to, Wiley."

He waved it off. "No, no, I have to make sure you're taken care of."

"That's very sweet of you." She gripped the back of the chair in front of his desk. "That's what I've come to talk to you about, Wiley. I need…I need some time off."

"Time off?" Wiley echoed.

"Yes," she said, pursing her lips. "Trinity needs constant care, and I need to be able to provide it for her."

Wiley picked a pen off his desk and twirled it around with his fingers like a baton. He pulled the string on the shades and opened them a little, gazing out into the front room. "I see."

"I know it's not the best time for this," Stephanie continued, "With the election coming up in a few weeks. But Trinity needs me."

"I need you too, Stephanie," Wiley said quietly. "This is the most crucial part of the campaign."

"I know, I know—"

He spun around to face her. "And you're the only one I trust to do it right." He took her hands in his, cradling them, enveloping them in his rough, calloused hands.

Wiley had worked so hard out west as a farmer with his father in his youth and when he'd moved to Halifax five years ago, he had no friends, only a passion for his fellow man. They'd met at a BBQ fundraiser for the NDP, and he'd had shown up with a white dress shirt and pressed pants. Everyone thought he was a member of the party the way he talked people up. But it was the way he talked to people that caught Stephanie's attention and drove her to overcome initial shyness to speak with him. He didn't just respond with a message track that some PR person installed in his vocal chords. He asked questions. He told stories that made people laugh and want to know more. He was relaxed and people could read him if they wanted to. No secret agenda. Just the pure kindness of a farm boy.

A year later, he ran for district councillor in the Quinpool area. Stephanie knew talent when she saw it and seized her opportunity. She volunteered to be his campaign manager and he won by a landslide. And the changes he made! The Commons, once unsafe to tread at night, now hosted weekly baseball games in the dark, lit by large stadium lights. Four years later, Stephanie had encouraged him to run for mayor. Wiley had said that if she could guarantee that he would win, he would pay her.

"You're doing great, Wiley," she said, squeezing his hands tightly. "You don't need me. The people love you."

"I'm not so sure about that," Wiley replied.

He released her hands and picked up that day's issue of the Chronicle Herald. Opening it to the Metro section, the headline jumped out at Stephanie. POLL: HODGES IN THE LEAD IN MAYORAL ELECTION.

"But...how could that be?" she wondered aloud. All this work, all this time she'd put into the campaign...

"I don't know. I thought the last BBQ went well," Wiley replied.

Stephanie held her head with her hands. She refused to cry, but she felt the tears fighting to be free to fall down her cheeks. "We're...we're not doing enough. What could we be doing more?"

Wiley was staring out the window at his volunteers, working tirelessly for him.

"This is the most important time for your career, Stephanie," he said softly, his breath steaming up the window. "When I become mayor—if I become mayor—I'll give you anything you want. I'll raise awareness for whatever condition Trinity is diagnosed with. I'll look into research that could help to improve Trinity's life. And you'll be there, my right hand gal, with me every step of the way. I just need to get there first, so that you can get what you deserve. What you need." He paused and glanced at her. "But…you should do what's best for your daughter."

Trinity needed her care. But Wiley had to win this election. He was what this city needed, with his strong anti-crime and get-it-done attitude. He could really make a difference. He could help Trinity have a better life! Maybe George wasn't trying hard enough to get time off. He was the vice president of an entire company, for Christ's sake! Couldn't he just take whatever time he needed, when he wanted? It would only be for a few weeks. George could take the time until then, couldn't he? And then, she could spend all of her time devoted to Trinity.

"You're right, Wiley," Stephanie said, trying to keep her voice even. "I'll stay."

He gripped her arms tightly, holding her close enough to him that she could smell his cologne. "You sure?"

She nodded. "I'm sure."

He drew her into a hug, pressing her firmly against him. She couldn't stop the tears then, and as she dampened his light blue dress shirt, he stroked her hair and took in her scent.

*

Ellie had been back in school a week longer than Zack. She attended her regular counselling sessions every second day at lunch and waited for news from him about Trinity. Every second of Advanced Calculus was dragged out longer than normal, and the equations morphed to look like the accident scene: equals signs became the road. Threes paired up to become chubby wheels. Fours became smashed windows. Sevens became bent Trinity limbs and eights became eternities that repeated without end.

The bell finally rang. Her unanswered questions became homework, but Ellie could not have cared less. She slammed the textbook shut with her questions inside and rushed for the door. In the hallway, she spotted Zack immediately. His black hair was gelled into spikes, and his white t-shirt and jeans—although slightly wrinkled, looked clean. The dark circles under his eyes betrayed his otherwise fresh appearance and made her heart tear at the thought of him spending sleepless nights being sad. She rushed towards him.

"You're back!" she exclaimed.

"Hey!" Zack said.

Ellie didn't know whether it was appropriate or not, and she didn't care. She threw her arms around him and felt his warmth. She'd heard from his parents when she'd called that he didn't shower the whole time he stayed at the hospital, but whatever smells he had acquired during his stay there were gone. His shirt smelled subtly of some sort of cologne, his hair of Head and Shoulders, and there was a hint of aftershave on his face. For one moment, Ellie breathed these smells in and pretended that he was hers.

Their lockers were located near each other next to the Advanced Calculus classroom. Zack opened his locker and threw his backpack—red with yellow stripes— inside.

"Your hair looks nice today," he said.

Ellie's smile went from ear to ear. "Thanks. I decided to straighten it this morning." She ran a hand through it to make sure it was still straight. "Um…so…how's Trinity?"

"I was about to go visit her, actually," he replied, closing his locker door and replacing the combination lock. "Her 'rents enrolled her in a special ed program here at school. She's in the resource room downstairs."

Ellie's smile dissipated. "Oh…well…that's good."

"Yeah. At least she's here, where we can still see her."

"Yeah."

She retrieved her sandwich from her locker and put her books inside, focusing all of her willpower on keeping her face calm. One of the books slipped from her hand and tumbled to the floor, its sharp corner knocking her in the leg on the way down.

"Shit!" she cried.

"You okay?" Zack asked. He knelt down to pick up her book, lying beside her left foot. His Jockey brand underwear peeked from beneath his jeans. Ellie tried not to stare.

"Here," he said, righting himself and handing her the textbook.

She smiled. "You're sweet."

He shrugged but returned the smile. "I try."

Ellie placed the book in the locker. "Did you want to take the rest of the homework I saved for you now?"

"You mean my mom didn't get it all?"

"She only came a couple of times. This is two days worth." Ellie retrieved a stack of about twenty papers and handed them to Zack. He took them grudgingly, and stuffed them in to his locker.

"Thanks. I guess I'll have to do them tonight."

"I can help you, if you want."

"Sure." But the sure was dismissive, Ellie thought. He could probably figure it out for himself—he was a smart guy.

"Pretty soon we won't have to worry about homework any-more, at least, not homework in subjects we don't like," Ellie said. She was desperate for conversation.

"I guess so, yeah." He rubbed some sleep out of his eyes.

As she replaced the combination lock, she formed her words carefully. "We'll be going off to university and all. Have you...?"

Zack sighed and shook his head. "Everything's up in the air right now, Ellie. I thought that maybe Trin and I would be able to do everything together, but now that she's..." He couldn't even bring himself to say it. He sauntered away from her.

Ellie followed him. "Tell me, Zack."

He lowered his eyes, and for a moment, he didn't speak. "It's like my world doesn't exist anymore. Like I'm in some bizarre alternate universe. Do you…I mean, I know that it's not exactly the same for you, but Trinity was your best friend…"

She bit her lip. "After the accident, I was so afraid that she wouldn't wake up."

"Me too," Zack admitted.

"But when I got that call from you, Zack…and I knew she was going to be okay, I started to feel better." She touched his arm. "Things are going to be different. We are going to be sad about it. But we can still do the things that we like to do, that we want to do. Graduate, go to prom—"

"I don't know if I'm going anymore."

"You're not going?" Ellie's stomach fluttered. The hallway seemed increasingly crowded and suffocating. Prom was the most important day of their teenage lives—besides graduation. It was the last time she would be able to see Zack dressed up, handsome…

Zack stuffed his hands in his pockets. "It just seems kinda pointless now, I guess."

"Because Trinity's gone," Ellie filled in quietly.

"Yeah."

This couldn't happen. Maybe he didn't know. Zack had applied for Dalhousie University, and had gotten accepted. Ellie had also applied for Dalhousie, but it wasn't her first choice in schools. Acadia University and Saint F.X.—both were sufficiently far away from her parents. Both were good schools with great kinesiology programs. She wasn't sure if she could afford to go to Acadia, which was one of the most expensive schools in Nova Scotia, but Saint F.X.—she could do that. Antigonish was a nice town, not too big, not too small. But it also meant leaving Zack and Trinity behind.

"Well…I think Trinity would have wanted you to go."

Zack looked at her inquisitively. "Oh?"

"Uh, yeah," she replied. "She was so excited for it. We bought our dresses last month. Hers was a golden yellow, dotted with tiny false gems and an under mesh that poofed it right up. And a tiara, I think."

"She would've looked beautiful," he said.

"Mine was nice too. Purple, and strapless," she added.

"I bought her a bracelet for a grad present. Guess I'll have to return it," he said.

Ellie paused. Was he listening to what she just said? "Yeah. I don't know if she'd know how to appreciate that now."

Or, she thought guiltily, you could find someone else to give it to.

They arrived at the resource centre. The door was closed and decorated with large coloured numbers and the alphabet. It looked like the entrance to an elementary school classroom rather than something you'd find at Citadel High. As Ellie and Zack drew closer, they heard raised voices coming from within.

Zack turned the knob and opened the door. Two of the resource teachers—Mrs. Bailey and Mr. Floyd were standing in the middle of the classroom, shouting at each other. Mrs. Bailey held a cordless phone in one hand. Although there were multiple long tables with chairs tucked beneath them, one was askew, as if its prior occupant had gotten up in a hurry and left. On the table in front of that chair were a bunch of blank white pages, a box of crayons and a black and red marker, strewn carelessly.

The teachers stopped arguing when they noticed Zack and Ellie. They exchanged guilty glances.

"Where's Trinity?" Zack asked.

"She's…she's gone," Mrs. Bailey stammered.

"Gone?" Zack echoed. "Where did she go?"

"We're not sure. We were trying to get her to draw, but she didn't want to, and then started fussing, and before we could stop her-"

"You just let her leave?" Zack interrupted. "What kind of bullshit teacher are you?"

"Zack!" Ellie hissed. She looked apologetically to the teachers. "Look, he doesn't mean it, we're really-"

"Yes, I do mean it!" Zack pounded a fist on the door, causing a bright red cut out of the number two to fall to the floor. "Why didn't you follow her?"

"We did, but then she lost us when she got outside. There are other teachers out looking for her. We're here in case she comes back," Mr. Floyd. "Listen, we just called her parents. They're on her way. Go and enjoy your lunch, and we'll take care of it."

"No!" Zack retorted. "I'm her boyfriend. You lost her, I'll find her."

With that, Zack stormed off down the hallway towards the exit. Ellie had no choice but to follow. She abandoned her sandwich on one of the empty tables and set off after him.

Citadel High was right next to the Commons, on Trollope Street, but the Commons was separated into two parts by Cogswell Street. The smaller part next to the high school had a playground and a skate park, whereas the bigger part, the main green space was commonly used for outdoor concerts or as a ball field. Cogswell Street was part of a large intersection on Quinpool Road—Ellie's stomach turned as she thought of Trinity wandering into traffic.

A paved walkway led them to the sidewalk where a road separated them from the grassy plain of the Commons. Groups of kids—mostly skaters—watched them as they passed, and Zack didn't hesitate to push anyone who was in his way while consistently screaming Trinity's name. Ellie maintained a safe jogging distance behind him.

The traffic wasn't too heavy and they crossed the road without much difficulty. Ellie could only imagine Trinity trying to cross the road. She must have been terrified, if she did come this way. Ellie looked up and down the street—no sign of her.

"Zack!" she called up to him.

He was far ahead, almost at Cogswell Street. Beads of sweat dripped from Ellie's brow as she broke into a run. Her legs burned, but it was a good burn. It had been a while since she worked on her cardio. She drew in a deep breath and called Zack's name again.

Finally, he stopped. They stood at the edge of the first part of the Commons and gazed across the street to the massive open greenery. There were people walking their dogs, and people walking solo, enjoying the sun that peaked out from behind the clouds. It was hard to tell if any of them were Trinity at this distance.

"I don't think she would've came this far," Ellie said as she caught her breath. "Do you really think she would've crossed the road on her own?"

"I don't know! I'm calling her name but she's not answering!"

"She doesn't know who you are!"

Zack raised his hand to slap her but stopped himself. He was frozen in some sort of heavy-breathing statue, looking down at Ellie like she had stabbed him in the heart.

She couldn't bear to see him like this. "I'm sorry."

A high pitched wail that sounded like a cat dying came from the middle of the Commons.

"Trin!" Zack yelled.

Ellie squinted. A cold dread seized her heart. Trinity had made it across Cogswell Street. She had been very lucky. Or, she remembered how to use a crosswalk. Ellie was going to use one herself, but Zack was off again. The road was a divided highway, with trees planted at the median. He sprinted towards Trinity's wails. Two cars sped down the road. Their brakes squealed; they narrowly missed Zack. He barely paid them any mind and only paused for a moment on the grassy median to wait for a break in the traffic.

She sighed. She wouldn't let him go by himself. His defiance of the pedestrian laws made her brave and reckless. As a blue van hurled towards her, she sprinted to the median. It honked its horn at her, but she paid it no mind. She was crazy. Zack was crazy. She was crazy for him. Adrenaline pumped through her as she and Zack raced across the second strip of road.

As their feet touched down on the Commons once again, Zack sped up and ran for Trinity. She shook her head, trying not to think about how out of breath she was, and instead focused on Zack's toned body zooming across the grass. He sprinted towards the sound, which erupted again, and this time longer and louder. Ellie hurried after him. She wasn't used to running this much and the cramp in her side confirmed it.

At last, Ellie spotted her. Trinity was stumbling around the middle of the Commons, making the same high pitched screeching noise repeatedly. She was wearing a long skirt with a white tank top. In her right hand was a wrinkled piece of loose leaf with some writing on it. In her left was a black ball point pen. From a distance, she almost looked normal, until she threw back her head to the sky and screamed. The seagulls passing by cawed back at her.

"Trinity! There you are!" Zack exclaimed. He rushed up to her with his arms outstretched.

She cowered away from him, almost drunkenly. "Can't... can't find..."

"What, babe, what can't you find?" Zack asked.

"The school, maybe," Ellie suggested between breaths.

"We're here to take you back, come with me." Zack held out his hand to her.

She shook her head fiercely, her black hair swinging wildly around. Ellie had gotten used to seeing her with makeup on, and now that it was gone, her face looked absolutely plain. No less beautiful. But plain. "Said it's here...but...ground... hard..." She jumped up and down, her black boots flattening the grass beneath them.

Zack tried again. "Please, babe. Come back with me."

"NO!" Trinity screamed in his face like a child, and then began wiggling her arms and legs around like she was trying to escape gravity and fly in the air with the seagulls. The piece of paper flapped in the wind and tore at the edges.

Ellie approached Trinity with the same caution you would give to a wild animal. She kept her voice sweet. "Trinity, can I see that piece of paper?"

Trinity's frantic anti-gravity dance came to a slow stop as she regarded her former best friend. She considered the wrinkled loose leaf in her hand.

"Please?" Ellie added.

"Ummmmmm," Trinity hummed for a while, shifting her weight playfully from one leg to another. "Okay."

She handed the paper to Ellie, and Ellie smiled. "Thank you, Trinity."

Zack scowled at her. "You're treating her like she's a little kid."

"That's what she is now," Ellie spat, and unfurled the piece of paper.

At first, Ellie thought that the black writing on the paper was scribbled nonsense. She looked closer at the tightly packed scrawl and began to recognize a few words. Must have been something the teacher wrote for her, Ellie concluded. She stole a glance at the ball point pen gripped between Trinity's fingers.

"What were you doing out here with this, Trin?" Ellie asked.

Trinity had found a puddle in the middle of the grass and squealed as she jumped into it, splashing muddy water all over her legs and skirt. A few drops stained her tank top.

"Trin?" Ellie tried again.

"Water," Trinity replied as a fresh bout of water flew up and got her in the face.

"Maybe we should stay with her, here. She seems to be happy," Zack said.

Ellie shook her head. "Her parents are coming soon. They'll probably want to take her home." She folded the paper carefully and put it in her pocket. Maybe the teacher would want it back.

"Want to go see your Mom, Trinity?" Ellie asked.

At the mention of her mother, Trinity's eyes lit up and she stopped splashing in the grass-puddle. "Mommy?"

"She's coming! Follow me!" Ellie said.

Trinity giggled and raced after Ellie as they headed back for the school. Ellie kept her pace slow so that Trinity wouldn't fall behind and lose interest, and continuously looked back at her, smiling, so that she wouldn't stop following. Zack brought up the rear behind Trinity like a brooding watchdog who wanted to be leader of the pack.

CHAPTER FIVE

The moon was full, and so it was time.

Edmund drew his large black hood over his face, and with his fellow brethren, walked across the Commons' dewy grass. It had rained for a few hours just after sunset, and according to the lingering dark clouds that threatened to block the moon, it would rain once more before the sun returned to the sky.

There was not a soul wandering around the Halifax Common—locally called the Commons—and Edmund had worked hard to keep it that way. His brethren patrolled the edges of the park, donned various civilian disguises, and kept the unsuspecting folk away during the times of meeting. There was no violence, not to the innocent and undeserving. Most of those folks worked hard for what they had and he respected that. So he paid them back in kind by keeping the grass clean of blood.

But to those that were Impure...

It had been what his father always taught him. *They're not our kind, Edmund. We might live among them, but that doesn't mean we got to like them. Sons and daughters of slaves is what they are. They were still rolling around in the dirt while we were farming the land.*

Their savage ways were confirmed when he was only seven years old. A group of them stumbled to the farm one night, reeking of booze and sweat, carelessly lighting smokes and throwing their lighters onto the hay by the shed. His father woke and went after them, but in their madness, the group stabbed Edmund's father to death and left his blood to feed the fire. Maybe it had dawned on them then that there might be more people around who had witnessed their crime, so they entered the house to loot and kill before the fire took it. His mother had heard the noise and rushed downstairs. The police later said that she had died of smoke inhalation, but not until she'd been raped repeatedly by the men.

Edmund knew. He'd watched the whole thing from the upstairs landing. Had he had made a peep, he would've been killed, but he was surprisingly cold and indifferent about it. After the men left his mother on the floor, dead or dying, he thought that maybe sticking a knife in one of their backs might make him feel something…anything. So he crept out the back—the fire raging in the front and about to enter the house—and saw one of them lingering, taking a piss in the rose bushes. The rest were nowhere in sight, but he could hear them not too far off.

Like a lot of old houses, there was a separate entrance to the basement, and it was open. Maybe they had thought there might be something valuable down there, and then abandoned it when the fire got out of control. Edmund approached the pissing man cautiously, dimly aware that the fire was closing in on them. The man let out a relaxed sigh, zipped up and turned around. Upon seeing Edmund, he stumbled backwards into the bushes, startled.

"Jesus," he said. "Where'd you come from…?"

Edmund said nothing. His father had taught him not to talk to strangers.

The man swore and drunkenly stumbled forward, looking for his friends and calling their names. His balance was severely uneven and he reminded the young Edmund of a twisty top on its last few spins, ready to topple at any second. It occurred to Edmund, quite logically, that he could be the toppler.

He ran up to the man and pushed him towards the open basement door. It was dark down there, and the darkness hid a steep set of stairs. The man fell forwards, shouting his confusion with his slurred speech. His head hit the top of the stairs with a loud crack.

Edmund still felt nothing.

Because the man lay in the middle of the doorway, now the door wouldn't close. Edmund couldn't have that. Even though the man was still conscious, he made no move to get up. Instead, he vomited over the stairs and himself. Oh well. The fire would take care of that too.

It was getting hotter. He had to hurry. It took him a few minutes for him to push the man completely into the cellar. The orangey hue of the fire was close enough to realize that the man's skin colour might've been lighter than he first thought, but at that point it didn't matter. The other men were dark-skinned. They had killed his parents and destroyed his home. His parents were dead. The statement didn't bring Edmund any grief, but it was very inconvenient. Where would he live now that his house had burnt down, with all of his toys gone? He shut the door with a satisfying bang. The man had gotten what he deserved.

Sliding the board that locked the door into place, he found he did feel something in that moment. A rush that bloomed in his stomach and then spread all over him to the tips of his fingers and toes. Better than a sugar rush...no, this made him feel alive. He had been in control of another person's life, and ended it. He felt like he could sense the caterpillars in the grass and feel the heat of the sparks of the fire a few feet away, and the approaching men, who by now must have realized they were missing one of their brothers...

He darted off towards the fire. The heat blasted his face and the flames licked his clothes, but the men wouldn't be stupid enough to follow, would they?

Edmund couldn't remember much after that, but someone must have seen the smoke and called the authorities, because they showed up shortly later and found him, hiding in the trees near the fire. The men had escaped by then. The rush had also disappeared, and he wasn't able to experience it again until he became a man, after years of being tossed from one foster home to another.

And now, he was here, in Halifax. And he had a plan.

With a Brother on each side, they walked towards the centre of the Commons. If one were to examine the grass closely there, one would find a green piece of twine. Pulling on that twine would make a slight, almost inaudible, clicking sound and the door beneath the wooden grass would unlock. There was someone on guard twenty four hours a day, seven days a week wearing a city construction uniform, in case a poor fool figured out the door. The fool would be assured that there was sewer construction going on beneath the Commons and there was nothing for them to worry about.

Although the Halifax Common was the oldest urban park in Canada and was originally used for the pasturage of military horses and livestock during the founding of the city, it had been settled long before that, but underground. Stretching beneath almost the entire park was a series of underground caverns and passageways that Edmund determined to be at least five hundred years older than Halifax. Perhaps an organization such as the Order of Purus had once dwelled there. Or perhaps the Mi'kmaq were doing something that the Europeans never knew about. Edmund was not much of a historian, and nor did he really care how the caverns came to exist. They served as an excellent meeting place for the Order of Purus away from prying eyes; unworthy eyes.

The Order of Purus was his creation, but yet it was not his main purpose in life. For the most part, it was easy to pull a quarter out of a man's hat and convince him that it had been there all along. Men wanted to believe that there was something greater than themselves existing in the universe. Edmund figured that he was fulfilling that need.

It hadn't taken long after his arrival in Halifax to find men loyal to his cause. He surfed the local chat rooms, hung in the pubs, and watched and listened for weakness. His first and favourite catch had been Linus. He had the look of a defeated man, his shoulders slumped over a drink in a downtown bar when Edmund had approached him. He fed the beast, buying him drink after drink, listening to his troubles—something about his wife leaving him, his business failing—nothing Edmund hadn't heard of before.

No recruitment would be complete without a demonstration of his god, Omnus. While Linus pissed his troubles away in the men's room, Edmund slipped a little something into his drink to make him more susceptible. He had picked up the drug while he was travelling in Vancouver—the dealers were so blitzed on the stuff that it wasn't hard to kill them and take mass quantities for himself. Normally, he detested drugs—they dulled the mind and the senses—but they did serve their purpose as a subtle way of persuasion.

It only took a small dose to win Linus over. As his pupils dilated and his mind melted, Edmund told him tales of Omnus, the one true god of the Caucasian race. All he wanted was to protect his people from the impurity of the other races, and those that sullied the purity of their own race. Linus listened and drank himself deeper into submission, and by the end of the night, Edmund was convinced that he was ready.

They made their first kill on Citadel Hill. It was a male prostitute, dressed in black leather pants and a low cut, v-neck shirt. Prostitutes were harder to kill than the homeless. The homeless were usually sleeping at this time of night, they were occasionally drunk or high, or they simply didn't care enough to try and fight death. Prostitutes were almost always aware of their surroundings, which is why Edmund had Linus distract the man—easy, considering his tipsy, drugged state. While Linus stumbled around the prostitute, Edmund struck from behind. Linus saw the blood, and he freaked and tried to escape, but Edmund knocked him unconscious. The drug would wear off soon and he had yet to bend the man to his will.

There was movement out of the corner of his eye. More prostitutes, or else, cops. Edmund picked Linus up and slung him over his shoulder—not hard, as Linus probably weighed about half as much as he did—and trudged down the Hill. The bumpy ride roused Linus and Edmund set him down.

"Run. They will kill us when they catch us." Edmund grabbed Linus' arm.

"Impure?" Linus asked, his mind still fuzzy from the blow.

"Yes. The Impure."

They ran further into the night, even when Edmund was sure that no one was following. Paranoia was the drug's longest lasting side effect.

Eventually they came to the Commons, the great park that stretched forever. A group of young men smoked cigarettes not twenty feet from them. There were only a few street lamps at this point, so the smokers were in darkness, but Edmund and Linus were completely illuminated. It didn't take long for the smokers to notice them and approach.

"They want to kill us," Edmund whispered in Linus' ear.

Linus breathed through clenched teeth, making loud, hissing sounds. His eyes were almost completely black behind his thickly rimmed glasses.

"Look at them. Some of them aren't even of our race. I bet they're carrying knives. They want our blood. They want to see it on their hands. They want to chop off our heads and display them like trophies. What are they contributing to society? Nothing. They want to seem tough, but we have a different power on our side." Edmund produced a dagger from inside his jacket and placed it in Linus' hand. "We must do our duty, or they will kill us."

The men were within earshot now. One of them, a six foot tall black man, the leader, walked before the rest and hailed Edmund and Linus. He reached into a hidden pocket in his jacket. "Hey, you guys got some—?"

Before he could finish, Linus pounced like a mad man just as the black man was going to produce a lighter. The dagger drove into the man's chest, all the way up to the hilt. Edmund had been right—two of the smokers did have switchblades on them. He made a note to get a gun in the future as they charged Linus. But Linus' senses were sharpened, and his paranoia made him run further onto the Commons.

Edmund, forgotten by the group, ran after them. He was a practiced runner and soon caught up with Linus, screaming like a teenager on a roller coaster ride.

"Give me the dagger," Edmund yelled.

Linus looked over his shoulder but in doing so, wasn't watching where he was going. He tripped and fell face first onto the grass, and Edmund, filled with the adrenaline of the hunt, skidded to a halt before him. The men were seconds away, and as Linus scrambled to his feet, Edmund noticed a rift in the grass—could it be? A...door?

He yanked the door open and snatched the knife from Linus. "Get down there."

Thankful for an escape, Linus obeyed. There seemed to be some sort of step ladder engraved into the wall, but Edmund didn't have time to examine further. The men were upon him. But Edmund was not afraid. Instead, he grinned, and laughing, stabbed the man nearest to him, twisting the blade deep into his gut before pulling it out again and manoeuvring to avoid a switchblade from entering his own gut.

He was outnumbered, and although he wasn't afraid, he wasn't stupid. Swinging his dagger madly in front of him to discourage the men from following, he jumped backwards into the hole. He almost didn't fit. Edmund squeezed through as a switchblade caught the side of his neck. Only a scratch, fortunately, but it hurt like hell. Edmund swung his dagger at the nearest pair of legs and pushed himself into the hole. He was right—there was a step ladder worn into the wall. He scrambled down as the first of many climbed in after him.

Linus was cowering in the corner, muttering to himself. "What do I do? What do I do?"

"We fight them," Edmund said.

Linus leapt to his feet, but the drug made him unsteady. Still, he was willing.

The two of them had the advantage. It was dark at the bottom, the only light coming from the moon shining through the hole. Edmund stuck his blade into a man's thigh as he descended into the darkness. He screamed, lost his footing, and fell to the ground. Linus smashed his face under his foot as Edmund made quick work of the next man in line.

The men fell down the hole like confused buffalo—white, black and Asian alike. Edmund and Linus stabbed and kicked and broke them until the ground was stained with blood and guts. A few ran off unarmed, perhaps smarter ones didn't venture down the hole and ran off—but Edmund was not concerned. Edmund found several lighters among the bodies and stripped off the clothing to create a fire. The tunnels seemed to stretch on forever. A perfect hideaway.

After Edmund shut the trap door, they burned the bodies. The smoke filled the tunnels with the smell of pork, and Linus salivated uncontrollably. The munchies, another side effect of the drug. This was going better than Edmund had planned. It didn't take much encouragement to break the greatest taboo held by man. Linus feasted until his belly was full, while Edmund chewed gum and watched with amusement.

That had been three years ago.

Since then, Edmund had perfected his recruitment and upped the theatrics of the Order. Hoods, rituals and fire—and results. One of the brethren with Edmund pulled the green twine. The lock clicked and together the three men hoisted up the grass that grew over the door. The man on watch, wearing the construction uniform, saw they were allies and climbed down the ladder to allow them room to enter the caverns. After his adventure with Linus years ago he had found an old, but studier ladder to make for an easier descent into the tunnels.

It was a five-minute climb down the rusty ladder to the bottom. The tunnel walls were lit with dim torches so they could see where to place their feet and hands. Once at the bottom, they each took a torch from a lineup on the wall and headed down the hallway, while the guard climbed back up the ladder and maintained his post.

They walked for some distance down the long hallway until they came to the centre cavern. It had a high circular ceiling that had been smoothened over the course of hundreds of years. Edmund fantasized sometimes that perhaps the previous tenants had utilized slaves to rub the ceiling smooth with their bare hands. There were traces of a dried red substance smeared in different places near the centre. Perhaps it was the Order of Purus' blood spilling instead.

In the centre of the cavern was a large flat rock that was indeed covered in the blood spilled by the Order of Purus. But it was impure blood from impure bodies that did not deserve to walk the face of the precious earth. Six brethren stood in a circle around the sacrificial rock, staring at the old, rickety man who had been chained there on his back.

"Please…please help me," the man begged.

"All in good time," Edmund said.

There was another rock-table a few feet to the right from the centre slab that housed the ritual knives. There were five of them, and when used on the victim in the proper order and manner, it cleansed the soul of the victim, and that of the wielder. Edmund gestured to the table and said to the man on his right, "Fetch me the First Knife, Brother Jasper."

Jasper limped to the table, retrieved the First Knife, and grunted as he struggled to return to Edmund's side. "The First Knife, my Brother."

He held the knife out to Edmund, and he accepted it with a nod from Jasper. "What happened to you, Brother?"

Jasper's breath was raspy. "I…I was in an accident."

"Why didn't you go to the hospital?" Edmund asked.

"It…it was too risky. I was carrying the ashes of the Redeemed in the truck when it crashed."

"Ashes…of the Redeemed?"

Jasper swallowed, his skin pale and clammy under his robe. "Yes, Brother. Forgive me. But you said that they had to be moved from our sacred space."

The stupid, stupid fool. Jasper was the weakest of the brethren, and it had been a moment of weakness in Edmund when he'd allowed him to join. Unlike the other brethren, who held day jobs at respectable organizations, Edmund was convinced that Jasper sat on his ass all day and received employment insurance for no reason other than he was lazy or incompetent. But he had seemed anxious to join their cause, albeit a little too eager to kill without respecting the reason for killing. Although the other brethren were silent, he knew their minds were racing with judgment. Now he would have to clean up his mess, as usual, to erase the doubts on the brethren's minds.

"Where are the ashes now?" Edmund asked.

"Washed away with the rain, I guess," Jasper replied.

He guessed. "That is not the proper way to dispose of the Redeemed, Brother Jasper."

"But it all ends up the same, doesn't it? I was just going to bury it in the forest off the highway, just like you told me to, just like I've done a hundred times!"

Edmund gripped the silver hilt of the First Knife so tight he was almost tempted to use it on his fellow brethren. But that wasn't allowed, unless he was proven to be Impure. He would look into Jasper, but later, he promised himself.

"If foul play was suspected in the accident, a forensic team will be on that site, even if it did rain," Edmund said. "Just like in CSI, men have ways of figuring out things, and if they pick of a sample of the ashes, they might just find human DNA in there. Then tracking the fingerprints left on the steering wheel will lead them straight to you."

"But…you'd help me if I was in that kind of trouble, right? I've been faithful to the words and wishes of Omnus, haven't I?"

The brethren exchanged quiet glances.

"Omnus helps those who help themselves, and me," Edmund said after a moment of intense silence.

"That's Jesus! He helps those who help themselves!" the old beggar cried.

"Jesus was a bunch of lies," said Linus. "Omnus is a real god. We have seen him!"

In truth, the men had only felt Omnus' presence. Edmund had seen to that. Whatever the men saw while on Edmund's drug only enhanced the experience.

"Brother Linus, please. The Impure man does not know what he is saying. He is lost, confused," Edmund said, rubbing his thumb along the dull side of the knife.

"We will Redeem him," Linus replied.

Edmund nodded. "You have spoken well, and for that, tonight you may be the Second Knife."

Linus smiled, showing off his perfect teeth. No doubt in the world above, he was a dentist. He had come a long way since that night three years ago. Now, he could kill without the aid of the drug. Edmund often wondered if the drug dulled the feeling guilt that men were supposed to feel. Not that he knew anything about feeling guilty.

Edmund assigned the rest of the Knives for the night. Each brother in turn walked ceremoniously to the table and retrieved their appropriate knife.

"How many sacrifices are required before your ascension?" Jasper asked.

"Sacrifices?" the homeless man squeaked.

"In order for my ascension to succeed, Omnus will require the blood of many Impure people. I estimate, once, or twice a week until the day of ascension," Edmund answered.

"Won't that be risky, to meet here that often?" Linus asked.

"The risk will be considerable. But the gain will be immense. Once I ascend, together we can cleanse the entire city." A smile tugged at Edmund's lips. "And the rush that Omnus gives you from one sacrifice? Think if we did five, ten sacrifices at once, the power that would create within you."

The jaw on each man dropped. Yes, he thought that might get their attention. They were all the same. It was either the high they wanted, or the women. Women, though, he couldn't control as readily as the high.

To the left of the centre slab was another table, similar to the one with the knives. This one had nine goblets and a matching golden pitcher, decorated with Greek symbols. In the pitcher was a dark red wine, almost the colour of blood. Edmund sauntered towards the wine table and poured a drink for each man. The hallucinogenic was a nice touch, and was masked by the sharp, dry taste of the wine. He was a man with many connections, and getting the stuff that was fast-reacting and fast-retreating was something for which he was willing to pay handsomely. It had been hard to find a steady supplier at first, but after a handful of trips back to Vancouver, he finally found a competent chap that Edmund paid well for his silence. The drug arrived every month to his home office, stuffed in various plush toys or clothing.

"Come and receive the offering from Omnus."

The brethren lined up and took a goblet, one by one. From the looks on their faces, Edmund could tell they were dying to steal a sip. None of them did, however. They all knew the story of the man who sipped before he was allowed, and had a nasty accident the next day involving a lawn mower and a chain saw that wouldn't shut off inside a locked garage. Omnus worked in mysterious ways.

Edmund raised his glass to the ceiling. "Thank you Omnus, for this offering. Now, let us drink!"

The men gulped down the red wine, licking every last drop from their goblets. Edmund tipped his glass and allowed the liquid to spill into mouth, but feigned swallowing. He turned instead and sauntered to the table with the knives, and let his goblet rest there.

"Ready your knives and open your minds to accept Omnus' power," Edmund said.

Those without knives took a step back from the table. The four with knives and Edmund stepped forward and surrounded the homeless man. Each held their knives above a specific location on his body. The First Knife, held by Edmund, was positioned above the throat. The Second Knife was above the heart; the Third, the right breast; the Fourth, the crotch, and the man who held the Fifth positioned himself near the left arm, for when it was time, he would move around the body and slit both wrists twice.

"Brothers of the Purus," Edmund began. "We are gathered to once again clean the streets of this unholy city and the soul of this Impure man. Let us return his blood to the earth, where Omnus purifies all."

The old man struggled against his chains. "Please, my name is Harry, and I'll give up my corner, if that's what you want me to do!"

At that moment, Edmund lifted his knife high above his head, preparing to say the final words and strike the Impure hard in the jugular. The hood on his cloak fell backwards before he had a chance to correct it, revealing his face to the homeless man.

"Hey…I recognize you…" the old man said. "Yer…yer that Dalton fellow, from the posters!"

Edmund quickly drew his cloak once more around his face. It was no matter, the tramp was going to die anyway. Him, and all of the other Impure in Halifax would be cleansed when he ascended to the Mayor's office.

"Omnus will Redeem you," Edmund said softly.

With one quick motion, Edmund brought the knife down on the homeless man's throat. Blood splattered everywhere as each man stabbed the Impure in turn, and oozed down the flat rock, adding new layers to an already existing paint job.

*

Mrs. Bailey had been working at Citadel High for the past twenty years as a teacher and assistant to the mentally challenged and to students with learning disabilities. Each one had sat at one of her tables, and no matter how resistant they were at first, they'd all eventually opened up and bloomed under her instruction and care. Most of them would never go on to be productive members of society. Many grew up and lived in homes with twenty-four hour supervision. But she ensured that each one graduated learning to read and write to the best of their ability.

After Trinity's unfortunate episode the previous day, Mrs. Bailey was unsure whether Trinity would be cooperative when it came time to sit and learn. To her surprise, Ms. Hartell escorted Trinity into the resource room with no resistance, and sat her down in the same chair she'd been in yesterday. When Ms. Hartell left, there was no screaming. No fit. She only said one word.

"Paper?"

Mrs. Bailey smiled at her and brought her some white sheets of paper and the crayons from the shelf above her desk. "Are you ready to show me your alphabet, Trinity?"

She ignored her and picked out a black crayon from the box.

"Do you know what colour that is?" Mrs. Bailey asked.

Trinity looked at her like that was the stupidest question anyone had ever asked her. "Black."

"Very good, Trinity. Now, can you remember the alphabet?"

Trinity's eyes returned to the blank sheet of paper. The new tip of the black crayon brushed against the pristine sheet, leaving a slight black mark in the middle of the page, before she started to form letters.

Mrs. Bailey waited patiently as Trinity wrote out the entire alphabet, pausing only a second between each letter as she carefully and neatly completed the task. When she was done, she slid the page across the table to Mrs. Bailey. She picked it up and admired it. Each letter was correct, and despite not having a ruler or lines to guide her, she'd managed to keep everything straight. They were written entirely in capital letters and although she'd taken her time, each letter had the shaky, unsure lines of a child.

"Excellent!" Mrs. Bailey said. "Now, why don't you pick a different colour, and we'll see if…"

She trailed off as she set the alphabet sheet aside. Trinity was bent over another sheet of paper with the black crayon, writing furiously. Her breath was quick and intense—in, out, in, out—like she was running a marathon. Mrs. Bailey could only watch for minutes as Trinity filled the page with tight cursive, leaving only a slight white margin and then discarded it to her right.

Not knowing what to say, Mrs. Bailey reached slowly for the paper. The writing was so dense she put on the reading glasses hanging from her neck.

The hooded men dragged Harry across the dew-sprinkled grass. The rain water felt good against the stab wound in his back but it wouldn't stop the bleeding. Even in the darkness he could see the trail of blood he left as they dragged him. If it rained again, the grass would be clean by morning.

"Trinity," Mrs. Bailey said slowly. "Is this a story you're writing?"

The girl didn't reply. Her hand moved the crayon without rest. The tip had quickly dulled and wouldn't last long without her stopping to peel some of the paper away to reveal more of the crayon, or for her to sharpen it. Trinity did neither. As if moving in time to a song that only she could hear, Trinity tossed the black crayon aside, slid a fresh new red crayon from the box, and went back at it.

Before long, a second, and a third page was finished. Mrs. Bailey was afraid to stop her. At least she wasn't running away. It was clear that her writing ability hadn't been damaged by the accident—but hadn't she been scribbling gibberish yesterday in a kid-like fashion, putting letters backwards and spelling words incorrectly? Maybe she was recovering her memory, but to make such a large improvement in such a short period of time?

Mrs. Bailey read the rest of the page and found that she wanted to read the second. The tale that followed in Trinity's newfound handwriting held Mrs. Bailey rapt, awestruck and confused. When her eyes had devoured everything that Trinity had written so far, she rushed to her desk to retrieve the cordless phone and dialled the emergency contact number, which was George Hartell's cell phone.

A man picked up on the second ring. "Hello?"

"Is this George Hartell?" Mrs. Bailey asked.

"Yes, who's this?"

"This is Mrs. Carolyn Bailey, Trinity's special resource teacher, from Citadel High. I'm calling about Trinity."

"What's wrong? Did she get up and leave again?"

"No, no, she's fine. But...she's writing."

George paused. "Isn't that what you're supposed to be teaching her?"

"Yes, George. But she's writing a story that's better written than last year's Giller."

CHAPTER SIX

Mrs. Shrimpton was a nosy old lady from across the street but she was the only person who would look after Trinity on short notice. It was a temporary solution, Stephanie told George. She often repeated it to herself throughout the day. George had not been pleased when she told him that Wiley wouldn't give her the time off. He hurrumphed and curled his lips, making his moustache hair touch his nose—was he ever going to shave that?—but he didn't push the issue further. At least there was that. Trinity had visited the hospital for some follow up tests since she was released; maybe he shared her hope that Trinity would return to normal soon.

When she arrived home that evening, she threw her heels on the welcome mat and hurried for the kitchen. Mrs. Shrimpton was spreading some peanut butter on crackers when she looked up and saw Stephanie. The lenses in her glasses made her grey-blue eyes look twice their natural size, and magnified some of her wrinkles.

"I was just fixing a snack for her. She's been keeping herself quite busy." Mrs. Shrimpton's voice was old and crackly.

"Where is she now?" Stephanie asked.

"Oh, upstairs. Staring at the wall. Earlier she was busy with her papers. Oh, I tried to get her to watch some shows with me, but she just wouldn't leave—"

"I can take care of that from here," Stephanie said, gesturing to the peanut buttered crackers. The sooner she got out of the house the better. "Forty dollars all right?"

After ushering Mrs. Shrimpton out the door, Stephanie raced up the stairs to her daughter's bedroom. How long had she been alone up here? Someone more specialized would be better at watching Trinity. Mrs. Bailey, perhaps. That would make George happier. She made a note to arrange something with the resource teacher later.

The top half of Trinity's bedroom was painted light blue, and the bottom half had white and navy stripped wallpaper. When they first redid the room when Trinity was eight years old it reminded Stephanie of a room for a little boy who was interested in navy ships. The only window was opposite the door and had no curtains, only horizontal white blinds. The hardwood floor was covered in the centre of the room by a spiraling hooked rug that Stephanie had bought during a trip to Cheticamp, Cape Breton. Her bed was unmade and papers were strewn all over her desk under the window, and on the rug. Stephanie stepped on a blue and yellow crayon as she entered the room. It crunched beneath her heels and bits of blue and yellow got lost in the folds of the rug. Where had *those* come from? She hadn't used crayons since…well, since before junior high.

Trinity stood, arms wrapped around her bedpost, staring at the wall. She seemed like she was in a trance and didn't notice Stephanie's entrance.

"Trinity, honey," Stephanie said, inching closer to the bed, while trying to avoid paper and crayon hazards. "How was your day?"

She didn't respond. The wall seemed to be more interesting than her mother.

"I heard that you were writing a story," Stephanie continued. George had called her at work, right in the middle of a staff meeting. It had been embarrassing but she told everyone to take five while George told her about Trinity writing some sort of brilliant story. Apparently Mrs. Bailey had noticed it first, and called him up right away. Stephanie had thought that that was an improvement, but perhaps an improvement that she didn't have to know about until she got home. She turned off her phone after that. Bending over carefully, Stephanie picked up one of the stray pieces of paper. The writing was neat and in cursive, written with what appeared to be a purple crayon:

"Omnus will Redeem you," Edmund said softly. He held the knife high above him before bringing it swiftly down on Harry's throat.

Stephanie grimaced. "Honey, this is awfully gruesome. Did you write this?"

Still no response.

"Well," Stephanie said. "Mommy's going to tidy up these papers now, okay sweetie?"

Silence, again. Taking her actions as acceptable, Stephanie began gathering up the loose pages and stacking them on Trinity's desk. There were fifteen pages total, written on single sided blank white paper with varying crayon colours. She tried to resist reading them, but found herself engrossed in the sickly descriptions of the ritualistic murder of a homeless man named Harry.

There was no way she could've written this. It was too graphic. Too complex for a girl with brain damage. Unless it meant that Trinity was getting better, and that the brain damage wasn't permanent. That would be good news. Then everything would return to normal. Still, writing about people getting murdered...perhaps it was a sick joke that Zack and Ellie were playing on her. If that was true, she would have to put a stop to that immediately.

"Trinity, I'm taking these pages downstairs," Stephanie said.

She grabbed them and straightened them on the desk.

"Don't touch that."

Stephanie's head snapped to her daughter. Trinity was still staring distantly at the wall.

"I'm sorry, honey, did you say something?"

Trinity's eyes moved to her mother's. They were no longer innocent; for a moment, Stephanie thought she saw a flicker of intelligence flaming inside the pupil.

"Don't touch that."

A genuine smile crossed Stephanie's face. Maybe she really was getting better! "I'm just going to put them in the basement, with the rest of your papers from school."

"No. Don't touch my story."

Stephanie began to feel wary as her daughter approached the desk. Her moves were slow; her voice had changed. It was angry and threatening in a subtle way that Stephanie hadn't heard before in Trinity, before or after the accident.

"But, Trinity—"

"It's mine," Trinity said shortly. "Give it back."

Stephanie was stunned at her daughter's command. "Trinity, don't talk like that to your—"

"IT'S MINE!"

Stephanie was so startled by the sudden outburst that she dropped all of the pages; they flew everywhere, and covered the floor like a light frost. Before she could bend down to pick them up, Trinity was already on the floor, scrambling, shifting through the pages and arranging them in a specific order. Stephanie watched anxiously as Trinity stacked the pages neatly, just as she had done, and held them close to her chest.

"It's mine," she said fiercely.

"Oh...okay, honey," Stephanie said slowly, forcing a smile. "It's yours."

Trinity turned away from her mother. She tore the blankets off the bed, and lifted the pillow. Carefully, as if she was handling a baby, Trinity placed the pile of papers under the pillow, and covered it with the blankets. When she was finished, she smoothed the wrinkles out of the blankets and smiled, proud of her work.

"It's like buried treasure," she remarked.

Her eyes had regained their child-like quality. No more intelligence—Stephanie's hope for Trinity's return to normality faded. Instead, Trinity scrambled off the bed and skipped out of her room. Stephanie peeked around the corner and watched her daughter thump noisily down the stairs like a six-year-old on Christmas morning.

That was weird, Stephanie thought. Perhaps her recovery would be a slow process. She decided to be happy with the outburst instead of puzzling over it. Trinity had made progress. If she recovered her social skills as fast as her writing skills, well, George would stop harassing her about being on Wiley's campaign, and she could focus on winning the election.

While Trinity played with some previously abandoned dolls in the living room, Stephanie headed for the kitchen. George would be home in a few hours. She should probably start on dinner. Out of the corner of her eye, she saw the answering machine blinking red. Three new messages. Stephanie pressed the playback button as she opened the freezer.

"Hello, Stephanie and George, this is Marisa Bendett from Dr. Letofsky's office. The lab sent back the results from Trinity's last CAT scan and a few other tests. If you wouldn't mind giving us a call so we can set up an appointment, that would be great. Thanks..."

There was a beep, and then, George's voice.

"Stephanie. I, uh…left you a message on your cell, guess you were in a meeting or something. Anyway. The doctor's office called about Trinity's test results, and I'm going down there after work. Give me a call, all right?"

Another beep. George again.

"Stephanie, it's me again. It's quarter to six. I…uh…went to the doctor's office."

There was a static silence and Stephanie waited for the message to end, but it didn't.

"Jesus, Steph. It…it isn't good. I don't wanna talk about it over the phone. I guess I'll just show you when I get home all right?"

Trinity was talking to herself in the next room. The message didn't end. His breathing was haggard as if he was holding back a sob.

"She's not going to get better, Steph. The damage is permanent. Our little girl…"

Beep.

The front door opened, and George appeared, holding a file folder brimming with papers in one hand, and the car keys in the other. Stephanie stared at him from the kitchen, her heart sinking in her chest. There wasn't going to be a temporary solution. It was not going to get better. Trinity ran to greet her father, but the sight of her like that only made Stephanie feel worse. She slammed the freezer door and swore.

*

Ellie had only been to Trinity's house a few times since the accident, but Zack was going there almost every day. During the times that Ellie would tag along—about once a week or so—she could tell that Zack didn't always appreciate her presence. He wanted to be alone with Trinity, but Ellie couldn't let that happen. She wasn't a seventeen-year-old girl anymore. She looked it, but she wasn't, and every time Zack tried to touch her to remind her that he was her boyfriend, she would shrink away.

And then when she wrote, she didn't want to see either of them at all.

Zack and Ellie would help Mrs. Bailey, since Trinity's parents had hired her to privately tutor Trinity a week or so ago. Mrs. Bailey would come for a few hours after school four times a week, instead of Trinity attending regular school. On one hand, it made Ellie happy that Trinity was receiving one-on-one instruction so she wouldn't be overwhelmed at school. On the other, Ellie was glad Trinity wasn't around as much, as it meant Zack's attention at school was undivided.

Well, almost.

It was almost like Zack was ignoring the obvious—Trinity wasn't going to magically be the same as she once was. But he seemed to take it as a personal challenge to get her to remember or re-learn as many things as possible, no matter how small.

"Trinity remembered her numbers up to twenty yesterday. We're hoping to get to one hundred by the end of the week," Zack said proudly.

It was the end of the day, and students were rushing to leave the building and catch their buses. Ellie waited for Zack, tapping her feet impatiently, as he retrieved his stuff from his locker.

"That's good," she replied.

"I know. Her speech is really improving too since you've seen her. She's speaking in full sentences now, mostly." He beamed as he slammed his locker shut. "Hey, did you want to come visit her today?"

His question surprised her. Not once had he asked her this in the two or three weeks he'd been helping take care of her. Maybe this was a step forward; maybe Zack did appreciate her company after all. Ellie couldn't imagine that hanging out with Mrs. Bailey was much fun. Maybe Trinity would remember something bigger this time.

Ellie twisted her lips. At the very least, she'd get to be with Zack…which was always a plus. "Sure, but I should probably call my dad to let him know."

"Use my cell." Zack took his phone out of his pocket and placed it in her open palm. She cherished the millisecond that their fingers touched, wishing it could last longer.

After letting her dad know her whereabouts, the two of them left the school and crossed the Commons to get to Trinity's street. They talked about school and homework and what they were thinking of doing on the weekend, but as always, Zack steered the conversation towards Trinity.

"So yesterday," Zack began, "Mrs. Bailey and I were helping her with basic math. She was doing really well, too. She even smiled at me a couple of times." He trailed off for a few moments. "But then just outta nowhere, she stops, gets this blank look in her eye, and runs up the stairs. I chased after her, but she was in her room so fast. She shut the door on me. Locked it even. I didn't even know she knew how to lock the door…" He had a sheepish look on his face. "It was awkward for a couple of hours."

Ellie raised her eyebrows. "A couple of hours?"

"Yeah. Just me and Mrs. Bailey, sitting on the couch. We watched TV." He shrugged. "Then, Trinity came back down the stairs. Like nothing had happened. I tried to get her to show me what she'd written, but in the end I had to go up and see it myself." Zack flung his hands into the air. "There were pages and pages and pages of writing, all over the floor, and her bed, and her desk...like a freaking hurricane had gone through there."

Ellie had only been around once or twice when Trinity had gone off writing. "Sounds like a lot."

Zack nodded, his almond eyes wide. "That was two hours worth. Mrs. Bailey said she only used to go in ten minutes spurts. It's definitely getting worse."

The severity of the issue was confirmed when they arrived at Trinity's house. Mrs. Bailey had been given the day off. Stephanie was sitting at the kitchen table, drinking coffee and rubbing her temples. The table was completely covered with Trinity's intelligent crayon scrawl, along with a file folder that seemed to be filled with Wiley Dalton's campaign stuff.

Fortunately, Stephanie didn't seem that fazed by Ellie's presence. She invited them to sit. "Can I get you guys anything?"

"I'm fine, thanks," Ellie replied.

"What's up?" Zack asked.

Stephanie pushed a pile of the papers towards Zack. "Have you read these?"

Zack glanced at it. "This is the story she's writing?"

"Yes," Stephanie replied. "I want to find out why she's doing it."

Curious, Ellie picked up one of the pages and started reading. The words were packed neatly on both sides of the unlined pages. "It's amazing. For someone in Trinity's state."

"Exactly. But she won't open up to me. I thought that maybe she would tell you why she's doing this."

Ellie pursed her lips. Stephanie wasn't home during the day, and her public speaking engagements with Mr. Dalton kept her late on certain evenings. She didn't see how Zack failed to bring back the closeness that once existed between him and Trinity.

She didn't see that even though Trinity sometimes responded to Ellie, it made Zack get this look on his face, like jealousy, but deeper than that, like Ellie was using something that belonged to him, like his guitar or his skateboard, and he wanted to play with it.

"I can do that," Zack said. "She'll open up to me, soon."

Ellie sighed, a little too noticeably. Zack shot her a glare. "What? Don't think I can?"

"No, no, Zack, it's not that," she said, waving her hand as if to rub the anger and sadness and pain off his face.

I want you to open up to me, she wanted to say.

Say it.

"I think that…that because of her…condition…it's hard for her to open up to anyone."

"Well, I thought that if it's not George, or Mrs. Bailey, it might be you two," Stephanie replied.

Ellie nodded. "How many of these pages are there now?"

Stephanie shrugged and reached for her work file folder. "Must be almost fifty. Maybe there's more upstairs. I saw a callus on her finger the other day, and it's only getting bigger." She slowly got out of her chair, holding Mr. Dalton's folder close to her chest, and ran her finger across one of Trinity's pages. "She's upstairs, but I don't think she's writing. She might be in a wall-staring mood today. So I wouldn't get your hopes up."

That's what's causing all this pain, Ellie thought as she and Zack collected Trinity's papers like robots and went upstairs. She was getting her hopes up that Zack would ever stop thinking of Trinity. It was like setting the chin up bar too high and then having the gym teacher expect you to hoist yourself up there. Ellie could do chin ups—but she couldn't do them when she thought someone expected her to do a hundred in a row, or two hundred. It was too much pressure. She prayed that some-day this hope wouldn't be unrealistic, but when they walked into Trinity's bedroom and she saw the giant smile that lit up Zack's face with a fiery glow, Ellie knew that it would probably be a long time before he ever looked at her that way.

"Hey, Trin, what's goin' on?" Zack asked.

Trinity sat on the rug, surrounded by dolls and stuffed animals. She wore a flowery summer dress that went down to the middle of her knee, but her hair was wavy and still slightly damp from the bath. A few crayons were thrown here and there over the floor, all of them worn and dull from writing. Her eyes darted between them, and then rested on the papers in their hands, looking like a mother bear who just found a hunter tormenting her cubs.

"Mine," she said.

Ellie set her stack down on the rug and offered her a smile. "Yes, we know. We brought them for you."

Zack followed her lead. "It's why we came. We want to talk about your story."

Ellie frowned and shook her head at him, making the throat-slit motion with her hand. "We can't just dive—"

To her surprise, Trinity interrupted her. "It...comes too fast."

"What's too fast?" Zack prompted.

"The...words," Trinity replied.

Ellie held up one of the pieces of paper. "These words?"

Trinity reached for it, but not in an "it's mine" way. Ellie let her have it and Trinity began to shift through the pages, lining them up in some sort of order. At first Ellie thought she was sorting by colour—all the blacks, all the blues, all the reds together—but then the greens interrupted that pattern and she placed them randomly throughout. Ellie touched Zack on the shoulder—he was warm, and her hand lingered there—and motioned for him to move back as Trinity expanded her sorting across the floor. When she finished, the fifty pages made a mismatched rainbow.

"That must be the order of the story," Zack said quietly. "Maybe she wants us to read it."

Trinity, bored after sorting, went to her desk and retrieved a colouring book off the stack that George had bought for her. Ellie knew he disapproved of the colouring books—they just encouraged her to act younger than her physical age. But she seemed to like them—maybe the repetitious act of colouring was soothing. Trinity shuffled over to her bed and rolled herself onto her stomach on top of the bedspread, legs kicking back and forth in the air, and opened the colouring book to an uncoloured page. Realizing that her crayons were elsewhere, she leapt off the bed—stepping on some of the pages in the process-and went around the room, collecting stray crayons.

Trying not to disturb the order, Zack and Ellie knelt before the first page of the story.

"I wonder if she understands what she's writing," Ellie said.

"She must," Zack said fervently. "Right Trin? You know what the story is, right?"

Trinity was back on her stomach, scraping a yellow crayon across the colouring book. "Story?"

"This, Trinity," Ellie said, not touching the pages but gesturing to all of them on the floor. "Do you know what it is?"

Trinity looked up briefly at them and then tilted her head back to her colouring. "No."

"You don't know what the story is?" Zack clarified.

She let out a frustrated grunt and threw the yellow crayon. It bounced off the wall in front of her and broke in half, part of it landing on her bed and the other part landing on the floor.

"Words...are...hard," she declared. "Too fast, not..."

She balled her hands into fists and began punching herself in the head. Zack reacted first and leapt to his feet, jumping on the bed and wrestling with her to stop. Trinity squirmed under his touch and kicked him in the stomach. He keeled over into the foetal position on the bed and Ellie rushed to his side, forgetting about the papers on the floor and almost slipping on them in her sock feet.

Trinity scrambled to the opposite side, pulling at her hair and muttering something inaudible under her breath. "Can't... no...stop..."

It was the first time Ellie had sat next to him on a bed. She caressed his left cheek—the other half of his face buried in the duvet— and she saw that he was trying not to cry.

"What do you want me to do, Zack? I can get you an ice pack? I can get Stephanie. Will you be alright?" The questions tumbled out of Ellie like an avalanche.

Zack's voice was strained and his eyes, teary. "Why doesn't she love me anymore?"

Ellie curled up beside him and took his hand in hers. He didn't resist.

"I'm here for you," she said. "Always."

They stayed like that for a little while, the three of them curled up on the bed. Ellie concentrated on Zack's hand: its warmth, the feel of his skin against hers. His eyes were closed but she didn't think he was sleeping. A single strand of his thin coal-black hair ran down his forehead and touched the eyelashes in his left eye. Ellie thought of brushing it away, but to touch his face...especially with Trinity so close...seemed like adultery.

Eventually Trinity's murmurings became quieter and were replaced by gentle snoring. The light from her bedroom window grew dimmer—it must have been getting close to six. Zack's eyes were still closed, and his left hand was still wrapped around his stomach. Ellie took a chance and quickly flicked the strand of hair out of his eyes, trying not to touch his face.

Zack's eyes twitched and slowly pried open. Ellie felt like she was an animal caught in a trap with her hand in his, her eyes wild with the thought: what if he pulls away, what if I'm doing something that he'll hate?

He rubbed his eyes. "Did we fall asleep?"

"Uh…yeah, we had a quick nap," Ellie said. She withdrew her hand from Zack's, immediately missing its warmness, and sat up.

Zack followed suit, running a hand through his hair, and looked over at Trinity. She was still curled in a little ball, hands covering her head as if something was going to drop on her from the ceiling. A string of drool escaped the corner of her mouth and landed on the bedspread.

"She looks…peaceful," Zack said.

"Yeah," Ellie agreed, shifting her gaze from Trinity to him. "Maybe we should get back to work figuring out her story?"

Zack shrugged and lowered his voice. "What's the point? She's sleeping."

"Yeah, but we could read it."

Being careful not to disturb Trinity, the two of them climbed off the bed and returned to the floor. A few of the pages had shifted from their mad scramble earlier, but Ellie was able to right them while Zack read the first page.

"The handwriting…it looks like hers," he said when he was done.

Ellie read a few random sentences from the second page. "Yeah, it does. But, how would we know for sure?"

Zack set the page down and stood up. He cracked his back and his knuckles, and then reached into the pocket of his jeans. He pulled out a folded piece of paper. It looked like it had been refolded several times and the ends were starting to fray. After a moment's hesitation, he handed it to Ellie.

"This is her handwriting from before the accident," Zack said.

Within

She unfolded the paper. It was list of things they needed to do for the presentation they were working on the night of the accident. Trinity's cursive looked like it belonged to a teacher, and she remembered teasing her that maybe she should become one because of it.

"It was the last note she ever gave me," he said sheepishly.

A sentimental guy. It tugged on her heart strings and made her want to move towards him. She drew her knees closer to her chest.

"But has all of her handwriting been like this since the accident?" Ellie wondered aloud.

Zack drifted towards the colouring book that had been forgotten on the bed and flipped through it. He stopped suddenly. "Look at this."

He crouched and passed her the Disney Princess colouring book. Above the messily coloured picture of Cinderella in her light blue ballroom dress, surrounded by sparkles, was the word "dress" in all capital letters. But the "R" was backwards, and so was an "S". It looked like the writing of a four-year-old who was just learning her letters.

"It might not be her writing," Zack said.

"It's her colouring book," Ellie pointed out.

They flipped through a few more pages. Above almost every picture was a related word, like with a picture of Belle reading by the fountain, the word "BOOK" was scrawled on top. Every word they found had backwards letters, or wobbly composition. Some were misspelled, and those ones had the correct spelling in neat red pen written next to them.

"Mrs. Bailey must have been using it to help Trinity with her letters, or doing word-picture associations," Ellie said.

Closing the colouring book, Zack placed it on the floor. "Then she doesn't write like this"—he pointed to the pages on the floor—"all the time. Just when she's writing the story."

"I guess so," Ellie agreed. "So that means…"

"Something creepy is going on," Zack finished.

Ellie shrugged. "Maybe creepy. Or maybe, it's like the TV show where people get second chances at life. Maybe this is Trinity's second chance to do something…worthwhile."

She thought Zack might argue with her about Trinity's usefulness to the world now that her brain was mush, but instead he picked up the second page of the story and gazed thoughtfully at Trinity's cursive. "Or what if Trinity is still trapped inside, somewhere, and this is her way of reaching me—us?"

So that was what he was holding on to. Ellie shook her head. "I…I don't know about that, Zack. People change when their brain gets messed up."

"Yeah, but that doesn't affect personality, right? Who she really is, inside?"

"Remember from psych class last semester? You know that any kind of brain damage can change a person's behaviour."

"Yeah…but she still has a soul, right? And this is Trinity's soul."

He grabbed the papers and shoved them in Ellie's face. She looked away, up at Trinity, who stirred and then stretched her legs out like a cat that had slept for twelve hours and was waking up for the evening. The real Trinity wouldn't have written a story, or coloured Disney Princesses. Maybe when her head went through the back windshield that night, another spirit had flown into her ears and taken up residence in her brain, and kicked the old Trinity out.

"Let's just read it," Ellie said finally.

They took turns exchanging pages as their eyes consumed the writing. The first few pages were about a homeless man named Harry, and a team of men that captured and then ritualistically murdered him with a series of knives. Edmund, who seemed to be the leader of these nefarious cultists, demanded that more blood be sacrificed to his personal god. During the day, Edmund disguised himself—as the mayor. The story alternated viewpoints between Edmund and the protagonist, another politician—a woman named Victoria—who was his friend. Their relationship wasn't clear to Ellie in the story yet, as she hadn't read that far. But the more she read, the more she wondered how on earth Trinity could conceive of such a complex plot and write such brutal murder scenes when before, she cringed at horror films and read only the classics for English class.

It only deepened the mystery and made her want to read more.

*

A line of sweat trickled down Edmund's face as he crouched in the shadows, waiting. It was 3 AM but it could've been high noon as far as he was concerned. The long sleeved black shirt that concealed the top half of his body, combined with the tight dark denim pants and the hoodie made him sweat something fierce, but it was necessary. The media was watching him like a bird of prey closing in on their next meal. They'd do anything to find some dirt on him. Fortunately he had had all the dirt swept up years ago. He was a clean slate, thirsting for blood.

He reached into his hoodie pockets and donned his leather gloves, turning his head away from the headlights of a passing car. It was a quiet night for Spring Garden Road, which made for slim pickings. Most of the hobos had been killed or had fled to shelters. He made a mental note to buy the homeless shelters once he became mayor and finish the ones that had escaped him.

So far tonight, there'd been a group of teenagers, but they were mostly white with a few Asians mixed in. Too much of a risk for too little of a reward. Then there was a group of three girls of darker skintones, but again, too risky. Perhaps if he had the brethren with him, but tonight he had his followers building cages in the tunnels.

The streetlights flashed red but Edmund crossed the deserted street anyway. It had become clear to him that his hunting days were numbered. He would have to be more careful, more subtle when choosing his victims. He could not have the good people of Halifax knowing his true identity—his true purpose in life.

So like any animal that hibernates, Edmund decided to stockpile his resources. Or in his case, his victims. The night before last, Linus and two other brethren had captured three prostitutes on Citadel Hill, and the night before that, there'd been a drunk Asian girl that had stumbled away from her friends only for a moment in the Saturday crowd at Pizza Corner.

She'd been young and hard to keep away from his hungry brethren, so he'd had to slip them an extra dose of the drug to keep them satisfied. He wouldn't have his men defile themselves by relating with an inferior woman.

He crept down Coburg Road and headed for Dalhousie campus. The street lamps were less intense there, less frequent. Part of it was residential, the locals completely unaware that their future leader was among them. There would be some good game along here.

It wasn't long before he spotted her.

His steps made no sound as the darkness of a side street consumed him. She passed under a street light, her ebony form casting a dark shadow over the sidewalk. Her hair was long and silky, tied back in a ponytail that hung over her backpack. She was wearing shorts and a low cut top that was just asking for trouble. Her face was slender, but her thick glasses shaded her face and he couldn't make out any other details. She was beautiful, really. Too bad she was of an inferior race.

Still…

He was surprised at his body's reaction to her and forced the vision of the men—the brothers of her race—into his mind. That quieted his cock quickly enough.

He waited thirty seconds and then slipped out of the darkness. His dark clothing was a decent camouflage, but Edmund had an appreciation for the natural instincts imbedded in the human senses. The girl tilted her head and hugged her arms close to her body, her pace quickening. She knew she was being followed.

They were three blocks from Spring Garden Road. If she reached there, he might lose his chance. At the next crosswalk, she hurried across the street. Edmund didn't dare follow her—that would be too obvious. He turned away for a few seconds to make it look like he was stopping for a smoke, counted to ten, and then darted down the nearest side street. His heart was steady as his feet pounded the sidewalk as he ran up the street, turned right, and then continued on until he found another side street that connected back onto Coburg. He was going to cut it close.

He lightened his steps and like an animal with no concept of traffic, he leapt out in front of the girl. Her doe eyes widened as she tried to flee, but Edmund grabbed her backpack and pulled her into him, wrapping his muscular arms around her scrawny neck. In one practiced moment, he had a knife at her neck.

"Don't scream, now," he whispered in her ear.

*

Stephanie awoke to a bloodcurdling scream.

It was coming from Trinity's room.

George snored away as Stephanie threw the covers off and grabbed her robe on her way out of the bedroom. George would sleep through anything; part of her begrudged him for that, and another part hoped it wasn't anything serious that she would have to wake him up.

Fastening the robe at the waist, Stephanie ran barefoot into Trinity's room. The door was open and the lamp light bathed the room in an eerie, yellow-green glow. Trinity sat on her bed crossed legged, head down, her hair splayed over a textbook and a stack of looseleaf in one hand. The other hand was writing furiously.

"Trinity, are you all right?" Stephanie asked hesitantly.

A sob escaped her daughter, long and high, but the writing didn't stop. Trinity looked up at her mother, tears streaming down her face. "Don't want to. I don't want to…"

Stephanie sat on the edge of the bed. Even though Trinity wasn't looking at the page, she was still managing to write perfectly straight, in cursive. She was sobbing uncontrollably, struggling to breathe. "Bad…things…"

"Shhh, it was all a dream," Stephanie said through a yawn. The digital clock said 4:13 AM. If Trinity could get back to sleep quickly, Stephanie might be able to squeeze in another two hours of sleep. She had a lot on her plate for today. Wiley was supposed to come over for dinner, and the house had to be in perfect condition; she had to make some important phone calls, and meet with the volunteers going door-to-door for Wiley…

She stroked her daughter's hair and took away the book that supported the looseleaf, throwing it on the floor. "Here, give me the pencil…"

It was a nightmare trying to pry the pencil from Trinity's fingers. It made tiny holes in the paper, now that the writing was unsupported. Eventually all she could do was take away the paper. Trinity continued to sob but she quieted as she slowly rested her head on her pillow. The pencil continued to move as it scrawled almost invisible words onto her sheets. By that time it was quarter to five, and she realized she couldn't leave Trinity alone with a sharp pencil in her hand, not in this state.

Leaving the light on, she crawled into bed with her daughter. Trinity stiffened as Stephanie lay next to her, but she didn't protest. As Trinity's breathing slowed and her eyes closed, her grip on the pencil loosened and then gave way. Finally. Stephanie slid the pencil onto the night table, turned off the light and settled back onto the pillow they shared. Trinity's hair tickled Stephanie's chin, but she made no move to scratch it. The early rays of the sunrise peeked through the curtains and casted a gentle glow on Trinity's face. Whatever bad dream that had once held her captive was gone. She was peaceful and vulnerable as a lamb.

She closed her eyes and thought, one hour, that's it.

Trinity gave a little contented groan and then snuggled into Stephanie's bosom.

"Loves you, Mommy," she cooed.

Stephanie's eyes opened, but Trinity was already fast asleep.

Chapter Seven

Ellie's dad dropped her off at Trinity's house just as the sun was lowering in the sky. She brushed her red pencil skirt off with her hands and took a deep breath of the evening air to calm her nerves. Zack was probably in there already, and she had some exciting news for him.

She'd been accepted to Saint F.X. That meant moving to Antigonish, which was two to three hours away. If she chose to go.

Her black heels made scuffing noises and pinched her pinky toe as she walked to the door. Zack had told her that Stephanie said to dress up, because she was inviting Wiley Dalton over. She had spent two hours deciding what to wear. She settled on the pencil skirt and a nice white sleeveless top—not too adult, but not too childish either. She'd even taken the time to apply mascara and some pink eye shadow. She hoped Zack would notice.

The dinner was for Mr. Dalton, to celebrate whatever success he had had on the campaign so far. Ellie hadn't really been following the election—even though she knew she should, since this was her first year of being eligible to vote—but she'd quickly browsed his website before leaving. He strongly supported the development of homeless shelters and job creation, and wanted to support Halifax's art scene. Those seemed like worthy causes. Ellie imagined having an intelligent conversation with Mr. Dalton, so intelligent that Stephanie would be impressed and Zack would stare at her all night and say, Ellie, I didn't realize the depth of your intelligence, please, I've been such a fool…

Zack answered the doorbell and Ellie grinned. He was wearing a button-up, dark grey dress shirt with thin blue and yellow stripes, and black pants. His hair was lightly tussled and gelled in place, and she thought he looked like a model for some fancy cologne or a higher end men's clothing store. Ellie's heart sang and despaired at the same time.

"You look amazing," she blurted out.

He gestured her inside and then shut the door. "Thanks. You too."

She looked at the neatly paired shoes on the mat by the door but decided that it would be socially acceptable to leave her scuffed up heels on. The house smelled like ham baked with cloves, and made Ellie's mouth water. When she turned around Zack was still there, staring at her.

"What?" she asked. She glanced down at her legs. She had remembered to shave this morning, right…?

"Just, uh…avoiding the kitchen," he whispered.

"Zack? Was that…?" Stephanie appeared at the end of the hallway, wearing a flowery apron over her white shirt and short black skirt. She held her hands apart, as if there was a sticky substance on them. Her face, once filled with excitement, drooped slightly when she saw Ellie. "Oh! I thought it might be Wiley."

"Nope, just Ellie," Zack replied. He glanced at Ellie and raised his eyebrows in exasperation.

"Would you two set the table for me, please? He'll probably be here at any minute!"

"Sure," Ellie said.

When Stephanie disappeared again, Ellie's stomach fluttered as Zack whispered in her ear. "Don't encourage her. Trust me."

I do trust you, her heart said, but her voice said, "What do you mean?"

Zack lead her into the kitchen. Stephanie was throwing together a rice dish and had several bowls on the kitchen counter, one filled with cranberries, another with some sort of white sauce, and another with walnuts. Ellie's stomach growled as the smell of the rice boiling on the stove and the ham in the oven joined in the air. If she were with her dad tonight, they'd probably just be having beans and defrosted garlic bread.

They didn't linger there. The napkins and cutlery were in the dining room, just off the kitchen. "Wiley likes to sit to the left of people," Stephanie told them from the kitchen. "Four years ago, we attended a press conference with some of the other district councillors. He answered questions better than anyone that day, including Caleb Hodges, councillor of District Thirteen! And he always claimed it was because he was on the very left."

Ellie caught Zack's gaze and rolled her eyes. He mouthed "crazy" and nodded.

"He'll tell the greatest stories," she continued as Ellie heard her dump a pile of something into the salad bed. "Have either of you ever met him?"

Ellie placed forks and knives around the table, which was adorned with two candles as a centerpiece, and a pristinely white, lacy table cloth. "I've just seen him on TV and stuff."

"Yeah, same," Zack echoed.

"You guys are eighteen, right? And registered to vote?"

If Trinity wasn't in the condition she was, and if she wasn't registered, Ellie suspected that she wouldn't even be there. "I am, yeah. Zack, are you registered?"

He finished placing the wine glasses. "Yeah. I think so."

"Great! The election is in a few weeks. The eighteenth of June," Stephanie said.

"The same night as prom," Ellie muttered.

"Oh yeah? Well, that makes it easy to remember, then."

The dining room and the kitchen were separated by an open doorway. While Stephanie finished preparing her dish, Ellie crept to Zack's side of the dining room. "Have you given it any more thought?"

"What, the prom?"

"Yeah."

He sighed. "You really want me to go, don't you?"

"Well…yeah, I do. It's the last time we'll see each other for a while."

"How do you know that? We'll have the summer, right? And I thought you were going to Dalhousie."

"I…I was accepted there," Ellie said. "But I got a letter today from Saint F.X. I was accepted into their kinesiology program."

Zack grinned. "Oh hey! Congrats! Come here."

He pulled her into a hug. Ellie buried herself in his shoulder. Why had she dangled that in front of him? He was happy for her. Happy, not sad that she was leaving. Might be leaving.

"You got accepted to Saint F.X.? Congrats, Ellie! I'd hug you too, but I have rice fingers," Stephanie said, wiggling her digits proudly.

"Thanks," she replied.

When Zack released her, he was still smiling. "So…you think you might go there instead of Saint Mary's or Dalhousie?"

Her stomach clenched. "I…I don't know. I could go to Dalhousie. Might be cheaper, to live with my dad…but I was looking forward to…you know, getting out on my own." She forced a smile.

Clouds seemed to slide over Zack's eyes. "We wanted to get out on our own, too…but…"

"Saint F.X. is a great school. I find the rings too flashy, though," Stephanie commented as she washed her hands. "Wiley said he went there for a while."

"That's…great," Ellie replied, not really knowing how to follow that up. Zack was straightening the wrinkles in the table cloth, his eyes absent. She desperately wanted to pull him aside and pull all of the grief and pain from his muscled body, but instead, she made herself step towards the kitchen.

"Wasn't Mr. Dalton from out west, though? Winnipeg, or Calgary?"

Stephanie dried her hands with a white and blue dotted dish towel. "Yes, but he said that that was when he discovered Nova Scotia's beauty, and decided he'd like to live here." She walked into the dining room and admired the table. "This looks great, guys. I release you from your kitchen duties."

"Hurray," Zack said sarcastically, and lumbered through the kitchen and down the hallway. Ellie proceeded more cautiously—she was more of a guest here than Zack—followed him into the living room.

George sat on the couch, wearing a dress shirt and nicely pressed pants, watching television. Trinity sat on the floor. She wore dress pants too—the first time she'd seen her wear pants since the accident—and a purple flowery shirt over a white tank top. Her raven hair was half pulled back with the help of a few bobby pins and a loose elastic band. She sat on the rug with her Disney Princess colouring books and crayons, ignoring the news in front of her. Zack collapsed next to Trinity, giving her a smile. Glancing up at him, she acknowledged his presence by passing him a crayon and a colouring book off the pile. Zack begrudgingly took what he was offered. Ellie, because she was wearing a skirt, opted for the lazy boy to Trinity's left, and turned her attention to the news.

"Although reports of missing homeless people are on the rise, there have been a number of missing young women as well, and many are suspected prostitutes..."

The news story showed pictures of Spring Garden, once ripe with homeless people begging for money, and the journalist talked to a few people on the street who said they regularly saw a man who stood next to the Shoppers Drug Mart. They always gave him money, they said, because he looked nicer than the others.

George scoffed. "Sure, sure, they look nicer, but—"

"Oh, Wiley's on!" Stephanie called from the kitchen. Her heels clomped down the hallway and then she burst into the living room. She turned up the volume as Wiley Dalton's face appeared on the screen with a CBC microphone pointed at his lips. He stood outside his campaign office on Barrington Street. Stephanie settled on the couch next to her husband.

"Well, I can't speak about the prostitutes," Wiley Dalton began with a charming smile, "but as for the homeless, the shelters are open and there to provide services like food and shelter for them."

"They aren't at the shelters, though. They're gone. What do you think about the notion of having homeless-free streets?" the journalist asked.

Dalton paused. Stephanie said something insulting about the journalist under her breath. Trinity looked up from her colouring book and stared intently at the screen.

"Healthy people are just as important as clean streets," Dalton responded. "If you or anyone is implying that something has happened to these people, I ask them to approach the police, because seeking justice is their department. Of course I'd like to see everyone with a home and a job, but unfortunately that's not how the world works. If I'm elected, I'll do everything I can to ensure that everyone is safe, including those less fortunate than ourselves."

"He's brilliant," Stephanie gushed.

"He's a liar," Trinity said.

Stephanie turned down the volume on the television and leapt off the couch. "Trinity, sweetie, what did you just say?"

Trinity bowed her head and gripped her red crayon so tight that Ellie thought it might break. She began stabbing the Disney Princess picture she was colouring in the neck, and sang, "Liar, liar, pants on fire, hanging on a telephone wire!"

"Stop that!" Stephanie ripped the colouring book from beneath her and slid it across the room. When Trinity wouldn't stop stabbing the carpet with the crayon, Stephanie grabbed it from her. "That's enough, Trinity!"

Trinity looked up at her mother, lips trembling. All Ellie wanted to do was hug her and tell her that it would be okay, but Zack got there first. She shied away from his touch and began balling her eyes out, covering her face with her hands as if she didn't want any of them to see her.

"He'll be here any minute," Stephanie grumbled. "I hope you're not that rude while he's here."

She cried even louder. "Mommmmmmmy!"

"Hon, Trinity doesn't know any better. You've made it worse by yelling at her," George said.

Stephanie sighed. "Listen, honey, I'm sorry. Mommy's just a little stressed, okay?"

Trinity sniffled but her sobs softened. Stephanie knelt and leaned forward for a hug, but Trinity drew herself into a little ball. Her mother wrapped her arms around her anyway, and Trinity sat trembling, staring angrily at the television screen.

The doorbell rang. Stephanie swore under her breath and wiped away Trinity's lingering tears. She turned to Ellie. "Could you get that, please?"

"Sure."

Ellie got up and went to the doorway. As she reached for the door, it jutted open, almost hitting her in the face. She stumbled backwards.

"Oh, sorry about that," the man said. He extended his hand and caught her before she could bump into the staircase.

Wiley Dalton was tall with intense green eyes, and his face looked thinner than it had appeared on television. He wasn't athletic by any means, but he was built with wide shoulders and a narrow waist. She could see the beginnings of a pot belly beneath his black button-up shirt, which were tucked into his off-white dress pants. The grip on her hand was firm, and he slid his hand down her arm. She felt goose bumps until he turned his grip into a handshake.

"I'm Wiley Dalton," he said. He had a slight drawl in his accent.

"Ellie Emerson," Ellie replied. "Nice to meet you, Mr. Dalton."

He let go of her hand. "Please, it's Wiley."

His hand was sweaty, she noticed. She waited until he wasn't looking and wiped it on her skirt.

Stephanie emerged from the living room. She smoothed out her short black skirt and felt her glittery studded earrings, as if checking to make sure they were still there.

"Stephanie, you look beautiful," Dalton said.

She blushed. "Oh, it's just the same top I wore today with a different skirt."

"George, you're a very lucky man!" Dalton shouted to the living room.

The couch squeaked as George got up. "You got that right."

The entrance hallway was getting crowded. Stephanie moved into the living room, and Dalton and Ellie followed. Zack introduced himself and shook Dalton's hand. Trinity had stopped crying but her cheeks were still a little puffy. She was staring blankly at the television like she'd been hypnotized by its moving colours.

"Wiley, you've met my daughter, Trinity, isn't that right?" Stephanie asked.

Dalton knelt before Trinity, blocking the television. "Hey, there. Remember me?"

"She doesn't really remember a lot of people from before the accident," Zack told him.

"Ah, I see," he said, rubbing his chin. "Does she talk?"

"Sometimes," George replied. "Usually only when you ask her something."

"How are you today, Trinity?" Dalton asked sweetly.

Her eyes flickered to life as they focused on Dalton. She bit down hard on her lip; Ellie thought she might draw blood. She reminded Ellie of a wild animal getting ready to strike. All she needed was the hair to stand on end on her back. Then Ellie saw the goose bumps on Trinity's arms.

Stephanie placed her hands on her knees and bent over. "Trinity, are you going to say hi to Wiley?"

"That's all right, she's probably just shy," Dalton said, standing up again.

Trinity's death stare continued long after Dalton stopped paying attention to her. Her face was as white as porcelain and Ellie was getting anxious just looking at her.

"The food's all ready, Steph. Is the table set?" George asked.

"Zack and Ellie set it."

"Well then, let's eat!" George declared.

They filed into the dining room. As to Stephanie's specifications, Dalton sat on the left hand side of the table, but to the right of George, who sat at the head. Stephanie seated herself to the left of her husband, across from Dalton. Trinity sat next to her mother, with Zack on her left, and Ellie was seated next to Dalton. The food was already placed on the table, covered and ready to be devoured.

"You don't say grace here, do you?" Dalton asked politely.

"Not usually," Stephanie replied. "Unless you want to do the honors..."

"No, I'm fine." Dalton lifted the lid on the scalloped potatoes and the smell and the steam came wafting out. "Actually, I'm starved. Let's eat."

Everyone helped themselves to a hearty meal, except Trinity, who had Stephanie to dish out her portion. The ham was tender and exploded flavor in Ellie's mouth. The potatoes were seasoned with butter, onions and enough pepper not to make her sneeze. The rice had too many cranberries for her taste, so she left it alone. George uncorked a bottle of red wine and poured some for Zack and Ellie.

"Now Wiley, you won't tell anyone important if these kids have a bit, will you?" George asked, winking at Ellie.

"Oh, I don't know..." Dalton smiled and winked at Ellie. "Think you can handle a glass?"

Ellie pursed her lips. "I think so."

"Thatta girl."

After everyone had wine, and George had poured Trinity some orange juice, Stephanie raised her wine glass with her pinky sticking out. "I'd like to toast to Wiley tonight. For his hard work and dedication to our community, and the entire city."

"Cheers!" George added.

Everyone except Trinity clanged their glasses together and took a sip. Ellie had tasted wine before, at her own family dinners, but this kind was dryer than she was used to. She set it back on the table.

Dalton took a sip but held his glass out once more. "Thank you. But really Stephanie, you do the hardest work out of everyone on my team. Whatever success I have, I owe it to you."

"*He holds the knife above Harry's throat and brings it down hard,*" Trinity muttered.

Stephanie's head whipped around. "Excuse me?"

"*Blood drips everywhere.*" Trinity's voice was more sing-songy now as she patted her scalloped potatoes harder and harder, until they were more mashed than scalloped. "*Blood, blood, blood, drips down the flat rock that doesn't get washed.*"

Zack and Ellie exchanged glances. They knew those words. They were from Trinity's manuscript.

Dalton lowered his wine glass. His face went from affectionate and genuine to cold and merciless in less than a second. Ellie noticed his fingers drift towards his butter knife resting on his plate, but his eyes remained on Trinity.

"Shh, honey, that's not very appropriate for the dinner table," Stephanie scolded, casting an embarrassed look at her husband. "Eat your potatoes."

Trinity leapt out of her chair, holding a knife in one hand and a fork in the other high above her head and proclaimed, "He will ascend and destroy us all!" She pointed her knife at Dalton like an accusing finger. "I've seen you underground."

"Trinity, that's enough!" George scolded.

Both he and Stephanie rose from their seats and grabbed Trinity by the arms. George pried the utensils from her fingers and threw them on the floor. Trinity tried to pick them up but her parents retrained her.

"Hooooooods!" Trinity cried. "Saw them..."

Zack stood and tried to shh her, but she only screamed louder. Ellie's brain raced a mile a minute. She glanced at Dalton. The empty, cold look was gone, but he was no longer smiling, and he stared at Trinity as if he was trying to dissect her.

"May I be excused?" Ellie asked. "I...uh...need the washroom."

"Of...course," Stephanie said in between Trinity's screams.

Throwing her napkin on the chair, Ellie concentrated on putting one foot in front of the other as she headed for the stairs.

Trinity had quoted the story. She'd referenced the evil killer who murdered Harry the homeless guy, and others.

She wrote it only in short bursts. When she was inspired. Possibly divinely inspired.

Wiley Dalton was a murderer.

The thought was so sudden she had to grip the staircase to keep herself from falling. It couldn't be true. It was just a silly story written by a girl who could barely dress herself and didn't know the difference between first and third person and couldn't, and wouldn't ever love Zack ever, ever again.

And yet...

The handwriting was the same as before the accident.

And the news, it said that homeless people were going missing!

And Dalton's reaction...that look on his face, a momentary flash of coldness, like he was going to reach across the table and wrap his fingers around Trinity's neck and squeeze the life out of her.

It fit together in Ellie's head like a puzzle piece, and the click sound was so sweet that it couldn't be anything but true.

"Ellie."

Zack came bounding up the stairs after her. She turned and put a finger to her lips.

"Did you-?"

"Yes," she replied.

They stood a moment in awkward silence, both knowing but afraid to speak it out loud.

"What do we do?" Ellie whispered.

Zack shook his head. "How do we know for sure if it's true?"

"We need proof."

"How are we supposed to do that?"

"Stephanie. She's the campaign manager. She has records, files..."

"That won't prove anything. If he's really a..." Zack glanced around his shoulder and lowered his voice even lower, "...a *murderer*, then I doubt it would be on record anywhere."

"It's a place to start," Ellie insisted.

"We'll have to follow his every move," Zack added.

"We could volunteer to help with his campaign."

"Both of us? Too suspicious. Just one. I'll-"

"Hey you two, ready for dessert?"

Dalton's booming voice ripped through their whispers. Surprised, Ellie let go of the handrail and dug her nails into Zack's shoulder. Dalton stood at the bottom of the stairs, wearing a toothy grin. In the lighting he reminded Ellie of the big bad wolf, and she was very sorry that she had worn her red skirt that evening.

He chuckled. "Did I scare you, Ellie?"

Ellie laughed nervously. "My, what a loud voice you have."

"All the better to give rousing speeches with, my dear," he replied.

Creepy, creepy, creepy. She had to remain calm. Ellie held onto the wall with one hand and forced her feet to move one after another, down the stairs.

"Speaking of speeches," she said as she inched her way closer to them. "I was wondering...well, I still need a few volunteer hours for grad, and I was wondering if I could maybe volunteer in your campaign office? Just a few hours, making phone calls…filing things…" Ellie's heart was pounding. She was sure he could see it through her blouse.

Dalton smiled and shrugged. "I would be happy to have an extra pair of hands."

Just like the hands in the scene where the hooded men light fire to the victim's fingertips and watch it sizzle and burn until it spreads down the arm and to the rest of the body, making the whole pit smell like burning meat? She was no longer hungry.

Ellie's face hurt from her fake smiling. She hoped there wasn't anything stuck between her teeth. "Awesome."

Stephanie came bustling down the hallway with Trinity in tow. She struggled against her mother's strong grip, screaming like a child at the top of her lungs, but Stephanie was taller than her daughter, and obviously immune to her tantrums. Dalton moved out of the way as Stephanie led Trinity up the stairs.

"Come on. Time to go to your room and think about what you did," she said.

Zack went down a few stairs to meet her. "Stephanie, come on, sometimes she doesn't know any better."

"I think she does," Stephanie challenged.

Ellie decided to seize an opportunity to be alone with Trinity. "You're right, Stephanie, she doesn't really know any better. Let me help you."

"Ellie! C'mon, you know—OW!"

"Sorry, did I just kick you in the shins? My bad. These heels are a bit too big for me." She smiled sweetly at Dalton. "Promise I won't wear them to the office."

He chuckled at her lame joke. See? Two can play this game, she thought.

Zack glanced between Ellie and Trinity and understanding lit his eyes. "Steph, Trinity doesn't really like it when you touch her. Maybe me and Ellie could try."

Stephanie frowned. Trinity continued to squirm, but was slowly losing interest. "She never minds when I touch her."

Zack froze. "Uh…"

Ellie rescued him. "What he means is that maybe she would respond better to non-physical encouragement to follow you when she's being punished."

She really wished Trinity had the power of telepathy, but she would have to make do with Trinity's heightened observational powers. Ellie held out her hand, palm up, and waited for Trinity's eyes to settle on it.

"It's okay, Trinity. I'm not going to hurt you," she said.

Trinity stopped struggling and caught Ellie's gaze. She almost wanted to try telepathy. Even though resentment swirled inside her like a poisonous gas, there was something else at work here, something that Ellie wanted desperately to believe. She felt compelled to connect with Trinity in some way, to let her know that she knew what Wiley Dalton really was, and to be a part of that otherworldly force that could stop him. She didn't think words in Trinity's direction. She sent feelings. Feelings of submission, of compassion, of righteousness. She balled up her anxious crush that she had on Zack and threw that in Trinity's direction too, because in that moment, it was just as big as her fear of Wiley Dalton.

It was stupid that she expected a response. She couldn't just beam her thoughts into Trinity's head, and she highly doubted that Trinity had the brain power to beam her thoughts back. Her pupils were large like full solid black moons, obscuring the iris so much that she looked like she was possessed. She stood, frozen in her mother's grip, until she reached for Ellie's hand.

"El…eee," she said.

Stephanie's mouth fell open. "Jesus Christ…she remembers you."

Ellie grasped Trinity's hand tightly, and she began to lead her upstairs. Stephanie slowly released her grip on her daughter.

Zack twitched and hovered around Trinity like a puppy wanting attention.

"Hey, Trin. You remember me? Zack?"

Her eyes swept over him, like a grocery store scanner swiping food, and then looked away. "Sad man."

"Well, this is a breakthrough," Dalton boomed. "This calls for more wine, I believe."

"Yes, yes, of course," Stephanie said. She trotted down the stairs. "I'm really very sorry about before, Wiley…"

"Don't mention it! Really, it's all right," he insisted. Ellie noticed how his hand found the small of Stephanie's back, just like Zack used to do with Trinity when they were walking together. "It's not her fault."

"I know, it's just been so hard…"

Their voices went out of earshot as Ellie, Zack and Trinity reached the top of the stairs and Stephanie and Dalton returned to the kitchen. The three teens went into Trinity's bedroom and shut the door.

Zack patted Ellie on the pack. "You did great back there."

"Thanks." Ellie grinned for a moment, savouring his praise, and then said, "Sorry she didn't remember you."

Zack shrugged. "I guess I'll just have to wait my turn."

*

Edmund left the Hartell residence that night feeling uneasy. Oh, pretending to be someone else came naturally to him, and he made it through the rest of the evening exchanging pleasantries and accepting Stephanie's dry wine, but deep down, he sensed that his plan was being foiled.

By a seventeen-year-old retard.

He kicked a large stone on the sidewalk, hitting one of the sides of one of the Hartell neighbour's cars. It created a small dent before dropping again to the ground.

Something would have to be done. Had the girl seen something she wasn't supposed to? What was the most vulnerable part of his operation?

Then he remembered.

Jasper.

That bastard was the one who smashed into their car that night. In the midst of his preparations for ascension and the stockpiling of the Impure, he'd forgotten. The vehicle was virtually untraceable back to him, since he had stolen it some years ago from a company that was going under and he kept it deep in the woods off the highway. Had the girl somehow seen the ashes of the Redeemed, and concluded...?

No, that was preposterous.

Had Jasper blabbed? Maybe. He was their weakest link if there ever was one.

If he was ever to ascend to the mayoral office, Trinity Hartell had to be taken care of. And he knew exactly how he was going to do it.

CHAPTER EIGHT

Every day after school, Zack and Ellie walked to Trinity's house and read what she had written that day on the manuscript. She was averaging fifteen pages a day now, sometimes twenty-five when she got going. Dark circles formed under Trinity's eyes; she must have been writing at night, too. Ellie couldn't imagine being struck with divine power in the middle of the night to write down the horrible urges of a psychopath. Perhaps Trinity was lucky that she didn't completely understand the meaning behind what she was writing.

Zack brought his laptop and began typing up the pages. Ellie sorted the new ones in the proper order. At first, they had assumed that she was writing the story chronologically, but new scenes appeared in the middle of the story that they'd already read.

Ellie had successfully infiltrated Dalton's workplace, but she hadn't learned anything new. She thought that maybe she was wasting her time, making stupid phone calls in a polite voice that sounded like she cared about politics. Laughing at his stupid jokes. When all she wanted was to get into his office and find something—anything—that would prove he was the man from Trinity's story.

Stephanie appeared in the doorway of Trinity's room where they were hanging out one day, arms crossed. "I hear you two are helping her with the story."

"Yeah," Zack said, glancing at her briefly before turning back to his computer screen. It's about twenty thousand words so far. You should read it. It's pretty good."

"I have read parts of it. Too disturbing for me." Stephanie said.

If only you knew how disturbing it really was, Ellie thought.

"Man, if the media ever knew about this…" Zack trailed off while he finished typing a sentence. "Trinity could get this published."

"Yeah!" Ellie agreed. If Trinity published the novel, the media would have a field day. She could see the headline now: BRAIN DAMAGED GIRL WRITES NOVEL.

But Stephanie shook her head. "Do you know how many calls I had to avoid from them because of Trinity's quick recovery? I already have to deal with them for Wiley's campaign. I don't want to have to answer questions about how Trinity's able to do this. Or why."

Trinity used her bed as a crutch to get to her feet. She had a piece of loose leaf curled in one hand. Her steps were slower and more careful than usual as she held out the page for her mother to look at.

"Thank you, sweetie," Stephanie said absently as she took the paper from her. She glanced over it and then frowned. "There's a woman in the story named Victoria?"

"Yeah. She's the protagonist, other than the murderer guy." Ellie replied.

"Hmm." Stephanie read the page more carefully and then set it gently on the desk beside Zack.

"Is that important?" Ellie asked.

"I guess. Victoria is my middle name." She smiled at Trinity. "Well, I'm going to make supper. Let me know if you'd like to stay." With that, she left the room and went back downstairs.

"Did you hear that? Victoria! Edmund is Dalton, and Victoria is Stephanie." Ellie said.

"Creepy," Zack muttered. "I think there's a sex scene in here somewhere."

Ellie's ears went red. "There…there is? I didn't read that part."

"She wrote it last night. It was the first thing I typed up today." Zack dug through some papers until he found the sheets, and then passed them to Ellie. She almost dropped them she was so nervous to take them.

"So…Dalton wants to have sex with Stephanie?"

"If this whole thing is true, then… yeah."

Ellie scanned the sex scene, but she was too shy to read it in front of Zack. Was Zack a virgin? She didn't want to know. She set it aside, by Trinity.

"So…you hungry?" she asked instead.

"Actually I feel like Thai food."

"Because you're Asian?"

"Yeah, pretty much. Though I'm Japanese, not Thai."

"I never knew that."

"More you know."

She giggled. "Well, I could go for Thai food. Where's good?"

Zack hit control-save on the Word document he was working on and then safely ejected the flash drive from the computer. "There's Ban Thai, but that's downtown. There's also this other place, it's a little far, on Spring Garden that's pretty nice. Trinity and I…" he trailed off. There was a moment of awkward silence, save Trinity scraping a crayon across the pages on the floor.

"We don't have to go any place that you don't want to go," Ellie said.

Zack breathed a sigh of relief. "That's good, 'cause I don't think I'm really ready to go back there yet."

"No?"

"No."

"I'm fine with walking a little further."

"That's good. We can always walk there and bus back. You got cash on you?"

"Yeah, I have twenty bucks." Ellie reached for her black purse, lying next to Trinity's dresser. "Even if I didn't, the bank's on the way, I could've stopped."

"Or I could've paid, and you pay me back. No big."

Butterflies fluttered in her stomach. Was this turning into a date?

Gathering up the papers and piling them neatly on the desk, and after packing Zack's laptop, they said goodbye to Trinity and her parents and went outside. It was almost seven on a Thursday night, and the sun was setting with magnificent blues and reds in the west, while the other half of the city already knew night time, with the stars watching over them.

"Nice night," Zack commented.

Ellie grinned. "Yeah."

Goddamnit, even if Zack wouldn't admit it, she was going to pretend this was a date. She would forget about Trinity for one night, if he allowed her, and would pretend that Zack had asked her out for a romantic stroll around the Commons and a delicious dinner at an expensive restaurant. She no longer wore tattered jeans, but instead a short, dark red dress, the colour of her love for him. And he would wear a fancy tuxedo, just like it was prom. And he would turn to her and say—

"That man looks really creepy."

Ellie snapped out of her daydream. They were nearing the edge of the Commons. A guy dressed in a jean jacket and sweats was leaning against a tree, smoking a cigarette. A backpack sat at his feet, half-opened. When they stepped onto the grass, they tried to walk around him, but he approached them instead.

"Hey sweetheart!" the man called out.

Ellie stiffened and fell behind Zack. "Let's go a different way," she whispered.

The man took a final drag of his cigarette and dropped it in the grass, putting it out with his foot. He glanced at Zack up and down. "What are you lookin' at, chink?"

Zack slipped an arm around Ellie's waist and pulled her away from the man. "We're leaving."

But the man followed. "Hey, I'm talkin' to you, sweetheart. You don't wanna hang around with chinks. They'll mess you up real good, knock you up with Asian babies. You want that? Babies with little slanty eyes...?"

Ellie tried to ignore the man and concentrated on getting to the end of the block, but Zack turned around to face their attacker. "Fuck off."

The man laughed. "Aww, he's standin' up for you, sweetheart, that's real nice. But why don't you let me take care of him for you? Then I can show you a real nice time."

"If you don't leave us alone, I'll call the police," Zack threatened, reaching into his jean pocket for his cell phone.

She didn't want to get involved with this, but it was too late. Although her heart soared at Zack's protective stance in front of her, the man leered at Ellie and made her stomach curl. He seemed unconcerned about Zack's cell phone, even when Zack flipped it open.

"Last chance," Zack warned him. His thumb dialled the number nine.

Ellie didn't know much about martial arts, but being a gymnast she often noticed how a person held him or herself. There was a particular stance that the body took when it was about to throw a punch. When the body moved, the head moved first. When someone was shifting their weight, they were at their weakest. As if in slow motion, Ellie watched the attacker throw his weight into his punch. She didn't even think about it—Zack was in the way, and he had to *MOVE*. She shoved him aside and kicked the man in the stomach. He deflated like a balloon and stumbled backwards, confused, and surprised.

"Feisty," the man growled, licking his lips and putting up his dukes. "You gonna fight me too, chink?"

Zack was picking up his cell phone and his laptop case. She hoped neither of them broke when she shoved him, just in case this got uglier. He reached for her, with a pleading look on his face—let's just leave, Ellie—when the man poised himself for another attack. This time Zack saw it in time. He ducked under the punch and ran onto the grass.

"Ellie! Run!" he yelled.

She wanted to run; her insides were shaking and her mind raced with the things the man would do to her if she were caught and Zack was beaten. But her body was ready for this. She did not tremble. Her breathing came easy. No one would hurt Zack. No one.

While the man took a second to decide whether to go after her or Zack, she somersaulted and landed with her leg extended. The force from the roll gave power to her kick as her foot rammed into the man's shins. He doubled over and gripped his legs as Ellie leapt away from him. "What the fuck?"

She back flipped—something she hadn't done in a while, and her muscles stretched painfully. She would pay for that tomorrow. Landing on her feet, she noted that the man was already on his…but not coming for her, he was going for Zack. Zack, slowed down by his laptop case, started to run, but tripped over a tree root jutting from the ground. The man laughed and latched onto Zack's leg. "I'm going to fuck you up, chink. And so will my master."

Terror seized Ellie's throat. This wasn't just any regular asshole looking for trouble. Didn't the manuscript say that Edmund's lair was somewhere under the Commons…?

Anger swelled within her. "LEAVE HIM ALONE!"

The attacker laughed some more and went to punch Zack again but Ellie came at him on the balls of her feet. Her anger and her fear and her love for Zack spun her around and helped her land a perfect round house kick in the jaw. The man bashed his head against the tree trunk and fell backwards onto the grass near Zack. While Zack scrambled away, laptop in tow, the man grumbled and groaned at his injuries.

"Fuck," the man muttered, spitting out a tooth. "Your girl-friend's good."

Ellie gritted her teeth. "I'm not his girlfriend!"

With one final blow to his nuts, the man groaned again and fell unconscious.

Ellie took a step back and suddenly, it all hit her. She just beat up a random guy. Well, not just any guy. He was going to hurt Zack.

Zack's jeans were covered in grass stains and dirt, and his small scrapes littered his arms, but all he could do was stare at Ellie. For once, she didn't want his attention. There was a bloodied—yes, bloodied, there was definitely some blood dripping from his lip onto the grass—man laying at the edge of the Commons. She glanced around—no one in sight, except some bikers on the other side of the field. No cops. No other guys. That she could see…

"Ellie…are you okay?"

He was beside her now. He touched her shoulder and she jumped, startled. Zack let out a nervous laugh and gripped her shoulders gently.

"You're okay now. Nothing's going to hurt us," he said.

She stared at him, into his kind eyes, and saw only…gratitude. She had saved him. If he was afraid, he wasn't showing it, not really. A trail of goose bumps hurried up her arms as she felt the warmth of Zack's hands.

"Where did you learn to do all that?" he asked.

Ellie was so caught up in the closeness of his face that for a few moments, she didn't answer. "Gymnastics since late elementary school. It just…it felt right."

He let go of her then, and it was with his release that she felt her tender muscles screaming from her lower back. She rubbed them, but it was going to be painful for her tomorrow.

"I knew you were in gymnastics…but I didn't know that you were…like, pro."

"No?" Her thoughts went briefly to the pile of cash Trinity had lent her to compete in the gymnastics competition.

"No."

"Well, more you know."

"All right, touché."

Ellie glanced down at the unconscious man. "Should we really just leave him like this?"

Zack shrugged. "I dunno. I guess we could. You were the one that really beat him up, though."

Ellie's face reddened. "You helped, a little."

"Yeah, a little."

"I guess we could move him under the tree with his backpack. Anyone who saw him might think he's sleeping and homeless."

The same dark thought crossed both their minds. Ellie didn't want to think about Trinity's creepy story as she and Zack took either end of the man and lifted him up. Ellie grunted, holding him under his smelly armpits as Zack held his legs. She walked forwards and he went backwards towards the tree where they first found him.

The streetlamp was behind the tree and cast a shadow over the man's body. Ellie checked again to see if anyone was watching, but no undercover cops jumped out to arrest them. She started to breathe easier. The man's chest inflated and deflated every ten seconds or so, so at least he was still alive. Even if he potentially worked for Edmund. Zack dumped him next to the backpack while Ellie retrieved the laptop case.

"Hey…what's this?"

Zack lifted the man's backpack and peeled back the half-opened compartment.

"Maybe you shouldn't be looking through his—"

Ellie trailed off when Zack pulled out a long, black robe. It was taller than him, with a hint of silver stitching all the way around the ends of the sleeves and the hem of robe. The hood had a thick red stripe running along the ends.

"Didn't Edmund and his pals have hoods like this in the story?" Zack asked.

"And they killed people in caverns beneath the Commons," Ellie added. "Hey…if we find the secret door to the underground caverns, would that be enough proof for you?"

"And how would we do that? Wait until midnight, until the rest of the clowns show up, and follow them under?"

Ellie shook her head. "Too dangerous. The story said that it's in the dead centre of the Commons. So we go there, and see if we find a green string."

"Oh easy. Just like a needle in a haystack."

"Zack! If this is true, and Wiley Dalton is a murderer, the whole city is in danger!"

"Just the homeless guys, and the prostitutes."

"No!" Ellie exclaimed. She felt like shaking him. "Didn't you read the latest scene? It's written in what's supposed to be his past. In the old place he used to live, he used to orchestrate elaborate kidnappings of teenage girls—all of them either black, Hispanic, Asian—anything not Caucasian—and murder them in the same fashion as these creepy, Satanistic stabbings."

Zack exhaled slowly. "So he's a racist bastard."

"Eugenics. He wants to create a pure world of white, probably blond haired men and women."

"Too bad he has brown hair."

"Maybe it's dyed. Also, Hitler had black hair, and he believed in Aryanism."

"Good point." Zack rummaged through the rest of the backpack and pulled out a flashlight. "Well, aren't you a tickle trunk tonight, Creepy Man's Backpack!"

Stuffing the robe back inside, Zack zipped up the backpack and switched it with Ellie for his laptop case. It was pretty dark by now. He flicked on the flashlight and a bright beam flooded the Commons.

Together they trekked across the grass, keeping the beam mostly straight ahead. They knew that if that man was an agent of Edmund's/Dalton's there would be more of them on watch. Ellie secretly hoped that all of them were as ugly and stupid as he was, and easy to beat up upon. The rush of finding out that Trinity's story might be true, and that she and Zack were putting the pieces together like teen sleuths—it restored her daydream of a romantic adventure. Quiet dinners in a Thai restaurant? The furthest thing from her mind.

When they reached what they thought was the centre of the Commons, Ellie knelt down and felt the grass. It was a bit wet from the morning's rain, and all she felt between her fingers were blades of soft grass.

"Nothing," she said.

Zack scanned the area with the flashlight and confirmed her suspicions. "Wait, the door was basically made of wood, reinforced with steel, right?"

"Yeah, I think so."

"Wouldn't it be hollow?"

Ellie grinned. "Yes, it would, smarty-pants."

Zack bowed and feigned a half-decent Elvis accent. "Thank you, thank you very much."

The two of them began jumping around on different spots of the grass. Each place they tried for the first five minutes was hard, solid ground, until Ellie bumped on something more hollow.

"Hey!" she whispered to Zack. "Found it."

He tiptoed over and pointed the flashlight at Ellie's feet. She knelt down and felt around the grass until she felt something rough and thin. She gasped, thinking stupidly that it might have been a snake or some other disgusting bug, but then logic took over and she wrapped her fingers around the twine.

"Ready," she whispered.

"I'll do it," Zack offered. He set down the flashlight and reached for the twine. His finger brushed against hers for a moment. In the dark, he couldn't see her smile. She lingered there for a moment, feeling his warm hands against her cold digits, wishing that he would take a moment to warm her hands before going after the bad guys.

"You got it?"

"Yeah."

She slowly let go of the twine and stood up. Her knees were

in line with her shoulders as she took a defensive position.

"Now," she said.

Giving it one hard yank, Zack managed to pull the hidden door up a bit, enough that if someone were walking alone in the dark, they'd probably trip on it.

"Again," she whispered.

He braced himself and heaved again. This time the door opened halfway. Ellie caught a brief glimpse of a man wearing a yellow hardhat. She thought she saw his eyes glint in the moonlight before the door slammed shut again.

The third heave yielded success. Zack stumbled backwards with the force of the pull and the guard wearing a construction outfit was ready for them. He hoisted himself up the ladder and gripped the edge of the grass. Ellie kicked him in the jaw, and his head bashed against the steel side of the door. Stunned, but otherwise undamaged due to his hardhat, the construction worker guard tried again to leave his hole and climb up onto the Commons.

"Take that!" Ellie cried, stuffing her boot in his face.

She thought she heard his nose crack as it smooshed against his face. He tumbled down the dark hole but not before grabbing onto her boot. Ellie screamed as she slipped, falling, her nails digging into the earth like claws as she caught herself on the grass. The man held on to her leg for dear life, pulling her further into the hole. Her arms burned; it took every ounce of balance and strength for Ellie to hang on.

"Ellie!" Zack cried. He knelt before her, his face centimetres from hers as he gripped her arms. "Don't let go, Ellie. I'm here. It's going to be okay. Kick him down."

She kicked but the man was holding tight around her legs. She heard others gathering beneath her and saw flames flicker in the dark abyss she was sure to fall into. The description of the tunnel came back to Ellie's mind, and the words that Trinity sang at the dinner table the other night haunted her: the slab of rock that ran red with the blood of innocents...

"There's a chink up there," the man shouted to those below.

"Get him, drop the girl!" another man's voice echoed up from below.

"No!" Ellie screamed, and struggled more, but the more she fought, the further she slipped, until only her head remained above ground. It was like trying to stay afloat in a sea of stormy waves.

Sweat poured down Zack's brow. He was pulling as hard as he could, but gravity was against him, and the man with the construction hat was heavier, stronger. Tears formed in her eyes as she stared desperately up at Zack, memorizing every pore, every shadow on his face. They were losing the battle.

"Zack...listen..." Each breath was a struggle. "I'm going to let go, okay?"

"No, you're not!" Zack shouted, his breath hot on her face. "You can do it. Pull...pull yourself up."

She shook her and gasped as she slipped a little more. The dirt was so far up her fingernails that it was torture. "It's not me they want."

Zack shook his head and gripped her arms tighter. "Can't... let you do that..."

A tear ran down her face. He was so stubborn, and she loved him for it. But he would never know. "Let... go...of me..."

She took a deep breath and relaxed her desperate grip on the grass. Each millisecond was heightened. Ellie cherished the look of desperation on his face, his determination—he would not give her up even if she asked it of him. But it was her sacrifice. She closed her eyes as she fell. Too many emotions made her throat tighten so she could not scream anything to him. He would never know she loved him since the moment they met, but with her sacrifice, somehow, she'd show him how much he meant to her. And he would live. He and Trinity would be happy. And if he was happy, then she could rest easy.

There was a crash below her, and a man's scream, and the sound of breaking bones. Ellie braced herself for such a fate, but she felt nothing but weightlessness. Perhaps she had died before the fall. She was spared the pain, and Zack was probably far away by now...

"Ellie! Pull yourself up!"

Her eyes snapped open. Her arms ached and this brought her back to reality and made her realize she was hanging in mid-air. She looked up, and saw Zack's face.

He hadn't let go.

Ellie's mind was numb—she thought she had died—but she obeyed Zack and slowly climbed out of the trap door entrance. The grass looked so comfy. Her legs buckled and she collapsed...but Zack was there, he pulled her up again. She leaned into him, both of them panting like they'd ran a marathon, the adrenaline pumping through her veins like a drug.

"You saved me," she said.

"We're even," he replied.

The trap door was still open. The sound of the men's boots clambered against the rusty steel ladder as they came closer to the surface. Ellie saw stars and her vision narrowed but she shook it off. "We have to run."

"I know." The flashlight blinked out and, after picking up their packs, Zack and Ellie ran for their lives. The men poured out of the secret trap door like a swarm of ants—how many people had Edmund tricked into following him? Ellie's heart pumped faster than that time she drank two Red Bulls while studying for her chemistry final. If she or Zack were caught, the consequences would be more deadly than a caffeine attack.

The packs slowed them down, but Ellie knew they couldn't abandon their evidence, nor would Zack want to part with his expensive laptop. A mental Google Maps came to her mind, suggesting escape routes and hiding places.

"This way!" Zack hissed.

He grabbed her hand and steered her towards him in the dark. She thought she saw another man coming from her left, but it was only a spindly tree. Zack called look out as a real man came at them from the right, and he steered them again to avoid him. They were almost off the Commons.

As soon as Zack and Ellie's feet touched the cement sidewalks, Ellie snuck a glance behind them. There were four of them, closing in, none of them wearing robes but she was sure all of them had come from the pits to make sure Zack and Ellie died—and painfully. No doubt they were hungry for blood and revenge for whatever happened to that man in the construction hat, and the man she'd beaten up at the edge of the Commons.

Zack slipped his hand in hers and led Ellie down one of the side streets. There were no street lamps there and trees overhung the sidewalks. They ran for thirty seconds and then cut down a narrow alley that connected to an intersecting street. Flattening themselves against the siding of an unfamiliar house that smelt like cat pee, they listened for the sound of their foes' footsteps. They were still there, but they were faint and confused. There was inaudible yelling made louder with the echoes of the street. Of course, that could have been some frat party. She prayed it was a frat party.

"My place is close," Zack told her.

She nodded and they set off running again. Zack lived on Lawrence Street, one street away from Trinity's house on Duncan Street. He led her to a basement entrance at the back of the house. Reaching deep into his pockets, Zack pulled out a key and shoved it into the lock. It clicked. The door creaked open, and he gestured for her to go inside.

The basement was an unfinished rec room with concrete floors, a couch to her left and a washer and dryer hidden under the stairs that led to the main part of the house. Pipes lined the walls and water gurgled through them as Zack shut the door and locked it quietly.

"Do you think we lost them?" she asked.

Zack flipped a light switch near the door several times. The light wouldn't come on. He swore under his breath about the light bulb not being replaced.

"I think we're okay," he said eventually, dumping his laptop case on the couch.

Ellie set the backpack down. "That was...interesting."

"Better than Thai food," Zack commented.

"Much, much better."

The scraping of shoes against the sidewalk startled Ellie once more. She drew closer to Zack, trying to keep her breathing even just in case the men could hear through walls. There was a small window to the right of the door that overlooked the sidewalk. Zack took her by the elbow and led her gently out of view, against the wall, as three sets of feet stopped near the window. Muffled voices outside argued with each other.

"Damn kids, they opened the door..."

"Edmund...not happy..."

"...Jasper, out cold..."

Ellie trembled and buried herself in Zack. She prayed that they would just go away, that Trinity would just stop writing about them so that they would stop existing, if that was how it even worked, or if not, for them to realize the errors of their murderous ways so that Trinity would stop paying attention. If only, if only she could enjoy the moment as Zack held her tightly, and not think about the men outside the door who wanted her dead.

"Zack," she whispered.

She cupped his face, and before she could think or speak another word, she pressed her lips into his. She didn't care if he didn't respond, but to her surprise, he did, wrapping his lips around hers, suckling them, moving his tongue into her mouth and intertwining it with hers.

Ellie barely felt the cold concrete as Zack laid her down upon it. He took off his sweater and balled it up to make a pillow for her head. She glanced up at the window; the men had left. Zack straddled her.

"You don't know how long I've been waiting for this to happen," she whispered to him as his face drew nearer to hers.

He stared down at her, caressing her face, moving her hair away from her eyes and lips. She couldn't see the expression in his eyes because of the lighting.

"What? What's wrong?" she asked.

He shook his head. "I…I can't. I'm sorry."

And as quick as it had started, Zack was back on his feet, pacing his basement, and running his hands through his hair. He scuffed his sneakers on the floor and sighed. Ellie sat up and took his sweater into her lap.

"I'm not a cheater," he said.

Ellie stood. She wanted nothing more than for him to take her in his arms again. "I know."

"This is my fault. Stupid, stupid!"

He punched the couch. It made very little sound, and Ellie realized this was probably smart as his parents were presumably upstairs.

"I should leave," she said, placing his sweater on the couch next to his laptop case.

She waited for him to protest, but he didn't. "I'll drive you."

"Are you going to tell Trinity?" she asked.

Zack hesitated and looked at her. "I have to, Ellie. She's my girlfriend."

"She doesn't know who you are," Ellie said flatly. "Don't you think you should move on?"

"Cold turkey, just like that, from her to you? Is that fair?" he snapped.

She swallowed. "No, but it's not unreasonable. I'd wait for you."

"Yeah? At Saint F. X.?"

"You know I'd stay here if you told me to."

"Don't be stupid."

"Go to prom with me."

"I…I can't."

"Can't, or won't?"

"Won't, 'cause I'm taking Trinity."

"Do you really think she'd be happy there?" Ellie asked. "With all the drunk people around her? And what if she gets the urge to write, what then?"

"I don't know! I don't have all the answers," Zack shouted. "I…I just want to know if she still loves me."

She opened her mouth to retort, but closed it again. There was no sense in insulting Trinity, or his feelings for her. Whatever he felt for her was obviously not strong enough, or Trinity was just this giant raincloud that wouldn't allow him to think about other potential girls.

And to think she almost sacrificed everything for him…

"Fine," Ellie muttered. "But she's not going to get better, Zack. I'm not saying that you should stop loving her. I'm saying that maybe you should give me a chance."

He didn't reply to that. He sighed, and then muttered something about fetching his parents, and went upstairs.

CHAPTER NINE

Edmund called Stephanie into his office the next morning with the pretence of thanking her for a wonderful evening the other night.

"It was no trouble at all, really," Stephanie gushed.

She was wearing a dark red lipstick today. Edmund wet his lips and thought about the First Knife, how it loved cutting into the throat and spilling the lipstick-red blood everywhere. But he wouldn't do it to Stephanie. Couldn't, really. She was everything that he desired in a woman, in a person worthy of walking the earth: her long legs, her work ethic, her fit body. He'd undo the clasp of the little cross around her neck and shove himself inside her on the flat rock, her body covered in the blood of the Redeemed...

"Wiley? You listening?"

Edmund snapped out of it. He was getting reckless. That retard had him distracted and off his game. He had heard about the little break in last night. Jasper had been careless and gotten his robe stolen by some teens. Somehow he suspected those two—Zack and Ellie—had something to do with that. One Asian and one athletic blond—couldn't be a coincidence. Ellie had conveniently finished her volunteer hours with him as well. The First Knife would have no trouble tasting the blood from her neck, even if she did not fit the usual criteria.

He put on his most charming smile for Stephanie. "Sorry. Just...thinking about the election. It's coming so quickly."

"Yes, it is. That's what I was saying, about the last big debate tonight before the vote. Our last chance to capture everyone's attention!"

Oh, their attention would be captured all right. "Yes, thank you for reminding me."

Stephanie nodded and turned to leave. "Was there anything else, Wiley?"

Edmund leaned back in his chair and twiddled his thumbs. "Why yes, actually, there was something I've been thinking about for the past couple days."

"What's that?"

"It's about Trinity," he said slowly. He had to be careful to word this perfectly, least not to arouse suspicion or invoke tears. "Does she always accuse the dinner guests of being murderers?"

A look of horror struck Stephanie's face. She tried to laugh it off. "No, no of course not! She was just a little upset before you came. I wouldn't worry about it."

"What would put such horrible words in her mouth?" Edmund pressed on.

Stephanie shifted her weight from leg to leg and sighed. She rubbed her temples. "She's been writing this story. A very awful, gruesome story about this weird cult led by this man named Edmund or something, and he tries to kill everyone, and some lady is trying to stop him..."

"Edmund?"

Saying his own name—his real name, the name that his poor farmer father had given him—that was something he hadn't done in a long time, not since he became Wiley Dalton many years ago to hide from his bloody past out west. Not that he wanted to hide. He would've liked to stay longer and soak in it. But the police warrants and rumours for reward for his death told him otherwise, and so he escaped to the East Coast, where everyone was trusting and friendly and would never believe that the good mayor-to-be had anything to do with murder.

"It is a brilliant story, well written, considering half the time she can't remember anything else."

"Fascinating," Edmund said, intertwining his fingers. "Do you know where the idea came from?"

"We don't know. The writing comes in bursts, and we don't even know if she knows what she's writing."

A real psychic, Edmund mused. That's what it was. Or perhaps God finally decided to take him on. Well, let them come—all of them. The police, the psychic, the Impure. They were no match for him and his thirsty bloodlust.

"I bet the media would love to hear about this," Edmund said casually.

"Oh, Zack and Ellie mentioned something about that too, but I don't know." Stephanie shook her head and smiled demurely. "I don't want to get Trinity to be considered a freak. The doctor mentioned that she would be prone to obsessive behaviour, so I'm sure it's just something that will pass."

"Mhmmm." Smart woman. It couldn't pass soon enough. If the media knew about it and made the connection, his life would be over. Edmund pretended to think for a few seconds. "Do you think Trinity and Zack and Ellie are going to the debate tonight?"

"I figured Ellie would be going anyway. Zack will go anywhere that Trinity goes...but I don't know, Wiley. She hasn't been in a crowded room since before the—"

"It's all right, Stephanie. I'm sure George will take good care of her for the evening."

She looked upset though. It was hard for Edmund not to be pleased with himself. The woman would bend over backwards for him, and if he wanted something done, she'd do it, whatever the cost. He was close enough to smell her perfume, and see the almost-invisible freckles lingering on her nose, and the worry line that creased her brow. George was a fat, hairy fool to keep such a prize for himself.

"Well...I'm not sure if George will be able to look after Trinity tonight. He does work late most weekdays." Her smile was hollow. "I suppose I could bring her...but I won't be able to watch her, I'll be too busy."

Women loved it when you touched them during the conversation. Edmund didn't know where he'd heard that before, but with Stephanie, he could feel the chemistry between them sizzle when he reached for her hand. A daring move, but she looked up at him with helpless eyes. She was his.

"Zack and Ellie will look after her. You can't keep her cooped up at the house all the time. Who knows, she may remember something from before the accident."

"Maybe...I suppose. I mean, she did remember Ellie the other night."

"It's good to be optimistic." Edmund pulled released her hands and spread his arms wide. "I see I've upset you. Quick hug, and then back to work?"

Stephanie wrapped her arms around him and squeezed. "Oh, Wiley. You're such a dear."

No, not really, Edmund thought. Trinity would barely make it past his speech, and then he would ascend to mayor, and no one, not even a psychic retard, would dare to stand in his way.

*

Zack couldn't avoid it. He felt like he was trying to stop time itself, dragging his feet on the floor. He didn't want to face Trinity after what happened with Ellie.

What had happened with Ellie? One moment they were running from Edmund's men, the next…she was in his arms. She had just smelled so good, and she was so tiny. Helpless. Yet, strong. She'd shown those guys what for, when he could barely punch them. He didn't know what had come over him. She'd just looked up at him, and her lips were so close…

And in that moment, he'd forgotten Trinity.

It was only for a moment, but it had been enough. How could he be so stupid?

He stood in front of her bedroom door. It was open. She wasn't writing. Ellie had avoided him for most of the day, and he didn't know whether it was because she was angry with him or because she was trying to give him space. He hoped it was number two, because he was a little number one with her. She knew he loved Trinity more than anything.

No, couldn't think about that now. He had to focus on what he was going to say to Trinity, and get it done.

Zack crossed the threshold from hallway to bedroom. Trinity sat on her bed, staring at the wall. So it was one of those days. He sauntered towards her, hands shoved in his pockets, and casually sat on the other side of the bed. He couldn't look at her. The bed creaked as he sat down.

Breathe in, breathe out. Breathe in. "Trinity?" His voice cracked. He knew she probably wasn't even looking at him. Probably wasn't even paying attention, as usual. Probably didn't even know who he was.

"I did something really bad last night," he started. "Well, it was good, because I found out that your story is true. I don't know how you're doing it. It must be really hard channelling all those words, all the pictures of the nasty scenes with Edmund and all his men with all those innocent people. Why you, though? I dunno, I'm just shootin' the shit now." He wanted to look at her. But staring at the center of the spiralling rug was helping him with his word dump.

"Anyway…I guess I should probably tell you the bad part. If you care. See, I was with…"

He opened his mouth to say her name, and his tongue wouldn't obey him.

"I did something with…"

Something warm on his shoulder. He looked over. Trinity sat next to him, her straight black hair falling over her beautiful blue eyes, her hand resting on his shoulder. His lips trembled as he stared at her, and thought of all that he had lost.

"I'm so sorry, Trinity," he whispered.

She brought her head down on his shoulder and rested it there, and he wrapped his arm around her and held her so tight he didn't want to let her go. He kissed the top of her head. It was then he realized that for the first time since the accident, she was letting him touch her.

"Trin…" he said.

Trinity lifted her head. Her face had a soft look, and the remaining daylight shining on it through the window made it glow, like she really was an angel. She slipped off the bed and went to her desk, and flipped through the stack of colouring books there.

So that was that. Done. The brief moment he had with intelligent Trinity was gone, and he didn't even tell her what he'd done. He just wanted to savour it again, pretend that the accident didn't happen. To say "I Love You" again and have it mean something to her.

Grasping her favourite Disney Princess colouring book, she brought it back over to him. She climbed up next to him again and starting flipping through the pages.

"Do you want me to get your crayons?" he asked.

She didn't respond. Sometimes that meant yes. He went to get up but she reached out for him again. He looked down at the colouring pages.

It was the Sleeping Beauty section. The picture was of Sleeping Beauty's prince, Philip, riding on top of his horse looking a lot like Robin Hood. Unlike a lot of Trinity's other colouring jobs, this one was neat and orderly, with no colours outside the designated lines.

Above the prince, written in all capitals and no backwards letters, was: ZACK.

It was childish, and silly, but Zack didn't care. "You remember me."

And then, a wide smile crossed Trinity's face. She took his hand in hers, and squeezed it tightly.

"Will you go to the prom with me?" he asked.

*

The debate, the last big push for candidates in the mayoral election, was held on the Dalhousie Campus in one of the empty classrooms in the McCain Building. They had people outside ushering others in, showing them which classroom it was in the maze that was Dalhousie campus.

Ellie arrived separately from Zack, Trinity, and Stephanie. One of Wiley Dalton's—or she should say Edmund's—volunteers directed her to the appropriate classroom. When she arrived, the room was set up with a snack table to the right, with rows of chairs in front of an empty white space at the front. A podium had been placed at the front as well, if any of the candidates needed it.

There were three people running for mayor that year. Besides Edmund, there was Caleb Hodges, who was another district councillor, and Rupert Stanley, who wasn't a district councillor but a prominent lawyer with a history of being active in the community. Both had strong platforms, but Stanley wasn't a charmer and Hodges wasn't a good speaker. Ellie had a feeling this event was planned around Edmund and played to his strengths.

She spotted Zack and Trinity talking to Stephanie near the front. She sauntered towards them. Zack was dressed up again, like he had been at the dinner party, only he was wearing a lighter grey shirt with his dark pants. Trinity was wearing a white summer dress that went just below her knees, and a pair of flats, which were probably safer for her to wear than heels. Her hair was lightly tousled, as if she'd run mousse through it just before she came. Even though she was mentally unsound, she still managed to look gorgeous. Zack must have helped her with that. Ellie crossed her arms and felt self-conscious in her black dress pants and blue sleeveless blouse.

"Ellie, so glad you made it!" Stephanie said, patting her on the back. "This is it, huh? The last hurrah before the polls!"

"Hurrah," Zack said lamely. "Hi Ellie."

Ellie noticed that he had his arm around Trinity's waist. Had he told her? She was letting him touch her. She averted her eyes. "Hey."

Before either of them had time to make an excuse to be alone and talk about their feelings, Edmund strutted up to them. He was wearing freshly pressed black pants and a white shirt with a blood red tie. The stench of cologne and toothpaste came off him so strongly that Ellie wondered if he had eaten garlic or killed someone before the debate.

"Hello all, thank you for coming," he said, nodding in greeting to each one of them in turn. She noticed he didn't single out Trinity this time. What was he planning?

Stephanie straightened Edmund's tie. "Wiley, are you nervous?"

He shook his head. "Nah. Just a standard win the crowd procedure. I'm going to get a drink before we start. Anyone want anything?"

"I'll have some water," Stephanie said. "Maybe I'll get it."

"No, no, I'll do it," Edmund insisted. He rubbed her shoulders. "You're more nervous than I am."

Stephanie smiled. "I'm fine."

Trinity scowled at them, and stormed across the room. People were starting to take their seats but it wasn't hard to lose her with her blazing white dress on. Zack followed her, excusing himself as he weaved between intimate conversations. Ellie took a chance and went after him.

"Look, Zack, I'm really sorry…"

Zack shook his head. "No, it was my fault. And…I told her everything. She knows."

His hand found hers again. She sat perfectly still in the back row like a doll, looking over each candidate like her life depended on it. At his touch, she turned her gaze to him and smiled.

"So…you two are…?"

Zack shrugged. "Obviously it's not going to be the same. There are still lots of things she doesn't remember how to do, and maybe she never will. But she's still Trinity, deep down. We'll see what happens."

Ellie nodded and sat next to where Trinity was standing. Her stomach felt weighed down, like she'd swallowed a pound of concrete. She didn't know whether to be happy that Trinity remembered Zack, or angry that he had chosen a girl with brain damage over her. She reached into her memory and thought of the one moment that he was hers, when their lips met and the world dissolved, and held on to that moment with all of her heart.

Stephanie approached them carrying a plastic cup filled with orange juice. She handed it to Trinity. "The only other drinks they have are coffee and water, and the water's almost gone. Here you go, honey."

Trinity took a long drink and wiped the extra orange juice on the back of her hand. Zack drew a tissue from his pocket and wiped the corner of her lips, smiling.

"We'll be starting in a few seconds, why don't you two find a good place to sit?" Stephanie suggested.

Zack and Ellie sat down next to Trinity while Stephanie sat in the front with the other candidates. The room was fairly packed. Broadcast journalists stood in the corner with their TV cameras. A few other print journalists and photographers sat in the front with their pens and cameras ready. People chatted in excited whispers about who they thought was going to win when Stephanie stood to do the opening address.

"Ladies and gentlemen, members of the press, welcome to the debate, the final chance for our mayoral candidates to speak about the issues that most concern Haligonians. Each candidate will have the chance to speak, and then there will be a five minute question period after each speaker. The first candidate is a personal friend of mine..."

Stephanie went on to give a heartwarming introduction for "Wiley Dalton" and Ellie didn't believe a single word. Trinity leaned against Zack's shoulder, her mouth slowly opening and closing like a fish that was eating invisible food.

When she was done speaking, Stephanie sat down again.

Trinity's pupils were getting larger by the second. She held out her hands and stared at them without stopping. So she was going to be in one of her strange, obsessive moods. At least she wasn't in the mood to scribble down more of her story. That would've been hard to explain. Ellie returned her attention to the front, where Edmund had risen to the podium.

He spoke for five minutes, and had the audience captivated. Ellie listened for the first little bit, trying to see if he'd hidden some subliminal eugenics message in his prose, but there was nothing. Nothing, nothing at all, it was just a normal speech made in a normal way.

"Don't...vote..."

Trinity's words were sluggish at first and only the people sitting beside and in front could hear.

"...importance of community, and that we stand together..."

"Blood, blood, everywhere, and not a drop to drink!" Trinity sang.

The people sitting in front in front of them turned around to give Trinity strange looks.

"...for we are a true community, united, and-"

Zack tried to calm her down. "Trin, what's gotten into you?"

"We will fight against you!" Trinity shouted suddenly.

Then, like some sort of out of control Amazon, Trinity screamed, leapt out of her seat, and charged. She weaved her way through the seated crowd at lightning speed, shouting curses and reciting lines from her manuscript until she reached the front of the room.

Within

She pointed an accusing finger at Edmund. "You are a liar!" Edmund glanced sideways at her and gave her a sympathetic smile. "Ladies and gentlemen, this is Trinity Hartell. Once a grade twelve honours student, she was the victim of a tragic car accident." Murmurs of sympathy passed through the crowd. Trinity shook her head and groaned. The photographers started snapping photos with bright flash that even Zack and Ellie couldn't handle to look at, and they were in the back.

Trinity began pulling at her hair furiously. "Too many voices...TOO MANY! Not listening!"

"If our roads hadn't been filled with pot holes and half-finished construction jobs, she would be graduating next week with her peers," Edmund continued. "Such a tragedy."

Ellie couldn't take it anymore. She leapt from her chair. "It wasn't just the pot holes. It was raining and a truck collided with us!"

More shocked gasps from the crowd. Stephanie twitched nervously in her seat while Trinity sat down on the floor beside the podium, staring at her hands once more.

"Which brings me to my next point," Edmund said, holding up a finger. "Driver safety. I will ensure that MADD presentations are mandatory in all junior high and high schools across the HRM."

"But I wasn't drunk!" Ellie protested.

"MADD is not just about alcohol," Edmund replied. "It's about putting the safety of your loved ones first."

Several nods by the concerned mothers in the audience. Ellie had walked into that one, and he had twisted it to his advantage. He had them. Mothers Against Drunk Driving isn't about not driving while drunk, you say? Ellie wanted to say this, and more, but Zack tugged on her sleeve. She sat down next to him while Edmund continued to drone on, imparting his lies.

157

"This is his arena. We're not going to beat him here," Zack whispered.

Trinity slumped down on the floor and stared at the ceiling like a hypnotized zombie girl. Whatever fire had been in her before was now gone. Stephanie's face was flush red. She tried to gesture to Trinity to get up without interrupting the rest of Edmund's speech, but she was like a limp rag doll. Zack was fidgeting, as if he wanted to get up and help her, but both he and Ellie wouldn't be able to make it to the front without making a scene either. Caleb Hodges took sympathy on the poor girl and quietly got out of his seat to help. He hoisted her up and settled Trinity on Edmund's empty chair next to Stephanie. Trinity's eyes widened as she leaned against her mother, as if she were staring at a ghost. Ellie frowned and leaned close to Zack. "Did you see that?"

Zack nodded, his eyes wide with jealousy. "She let Hodges touch her."

"She's never acted like that before. Look at her panting, like a dog."

She was sure they were both thinking the same thing. Ellie bent over and retrieved the empty glass of orange juice. Being careful not to touch the rim, she smelled it.

"I don't know…this doesn't really smell like orange juice," Ellie whispered.

She passed it to Zack. He had a whiff. He shook his head. "I don't know. We'd have to get it tested to know for sure."

Ellie took it back from him and carefully placed it in her purse. "But how…?"

"I will now take any questions," Edmund said.

Trinity suddenly and violently vomited on the floor. At first the retching sound stunned the room into silence, but as soon as it hit the floor Stephanie was out of her seat and barking directions at random people: "Get that pile of napkins from the table! Edmund, keep talking. Point that camera at Edmund or you'll have a lawsuit on your hands!"

While some people with weak stomachs fled the room, more cameras flashed. Stephanie, holding Trinity under her arms, cursed at the journalists. "No more pictures! You need release forms to print those!"

The stench of vomit was strong and several people got up to leave; some held in their own barf, trying to find a washroom. Zack pushed his way through the crowd and made it to the front, with Ellie following in his wake. Ellie had never seen her friend throw up. Once radiant even in her innocence, Trinity was back to being a broken child in a teenager's body. She buried her face in her hands and sobbed loudly, her ears red with shame. Cameras flashed and captured the scene for eternity. The headlines were already being discussed. Crazed Mentally Challenged Girl Out of Control During Mayoral Debates.

She didn't deserve this. No one did.

"Take her. I can't leave," Stephanie said curtly to Zack.

Trinity fell into his arms as she cried saliva and dribbles of vomit on his shoulder. Zack kissed her forehead and rocked her gently, but his eyes strayed to Ellie and made his thoughts clear.

Edmund had done this. Oh, he had a concerned look on his face as Stephanie stepped in front of the cameras and tried to usher them out of the room, and appeared calm as he had a private conversation with Caleb Hodges. But he was completely guilty. He had drugged poor Trinity and he would pay dearly. If only they could tell those journalists the truth of what he was, the monster that lay deep inside that reared its ugly head to the unfortunate few that felt his knives.

Chapter Ten

Everything Stephanie had worked for had been ruined by her daughter. It wasn't her fault, people had come up to her and said. Poor dear, that's horrible what happened to her. Maybe you should put her on medication for that terrible screeching. Trinity had embarrassed her as a campaign manager, and as a mother.

On the drive home she was seething. She didn't even bother to drop off Zack and Ellie. She parked in the driveway, got out of the car and stormed into the house. She just needed a moment to calm down, some sort of escape. This was one of those rare moments she wished she hadn't given up smoking.

George was working at his laptop in the living room. "How'd it go, honey?"

She muttered something nonsensical under her breath, and pulled at her hair when Zack, Trinity and Ellie came through the door. She had to remain calm. She had to find out for sure what was wrong with Trinity.

Taking a deep breath, Stephanie put on a sweet smile and sauntered over to the three teens. "Trinity, sweetie, want to come upstairs with Mommy for a minute?"

The vomit had been cleaned off her face, and she now smelled like a mix of barf and fresh bathroom soap. She could walk on her own now, too; Zack and Ellie let go of her and she followed Stephanie slowly up the stairs. Trinity clenched and unclenched her jaw and her teeth made loud grinding noises as she followed her mother into her bedroom.

Stephanie shut the door behind Trinity. "What has gotten into you?"

Trinity continued to grind her teeth and went to the window, plastering her face against it. Drool dripped down the pane.

Stephanie couldn't take it anymore. She grabbed Trinity and forced her to turn around and face her. "What is wrong with you? Why are you like this?"

"Mommy," Trinity said. Her voice was lazy. "Stop."

"No, you stop!" Stephanie shook her as if it would get rid of the retardedness rooted in her brain. "Where did you get the idea for that filthy story? TELL ME!"

Trinity started to cry. Her wail was like that of a small child. She reached out with wet, drool-soaked fingers and clasped the silver cross the Stephanie wore around her neck. The chain dug into the back of Stephanie's neck and she gasped as it snapped in two. Trinity held the tiny Jesus nailed to the cross in her palm and then dangled it in front of her mother's face.

"WHY WON'T YOU LISTEN?" she screamed.

Stunned, Stephanie let go of her daughter. Trinity sobbed. The cross swung lightly back and forth.

"Trinity...are you trying to say that...?"

"I listen," Trinity said simply.

She heard Zack and Ellie bound up the stairs, with George close behind. They waited in the doorway, as if the cross wouldn't allow them to enter. Stephanie, confused and angry and filled with a strange joy that her daughter was holding Jesus, said, "Is this part of some greater plan?"

"It's all true, Stephanie," Zack said. "Everything in the story she wrote is true."

Stephanie whirled around to face them. "True...?"

The words that tumbled out of Zack and Ellie seemed just as made up as Trinity's story. Hooded men killing people. That their leader, Edmund, was actually Wiley. To think that Wiley would hurt anyone...impossible. He was gentle and kind...especially to her.

"You don't have any proof!" Stephanie shouted. "You...you could've made her write those things, put the ideas in her head!"

"You've seen her in her writing frenzies. We didn't do anything," Ellie said. "And we do have proof. We found a hood, exactly like the ones Trinity described, on men that she described guarding the same places as in the story. And the trap door was exactly where she said. Haven't you been listening to the news? People have been disappearing. Ever ask Dalton what he does with his free nights?"

"He is a good man. He's a simple farmer's son who came to Halifax to make a difference."

"Try Googling him. There's no record of him before he came here. But there is a string of murders out west by a man named Edmund, just like Trinity described."

"She must have read it on the internet before the accident, and now she's channelling the information, somehow," Stephanie said. "That's the only reasonable explanation."

"We'll show you the trap door," Zack offered. "Then would you believe us?"

Stephanie looked to her husband pleadingly. "George..."

"I've read the story, Steph. I know it sounds crazy. And maybe Trin did know all these things before and know she's weaving it into some fantastical tale. But she never showed any interest in Wiley before this, and I think maybe we should give the kids a chance to prove themselves. What's the harm in that?"

"Harm?" Stephanie shook her head. "My career is what will get harmed! If the media were to get a hold of this…this… association…he won't be elected mayor, and I'll go back to being nobody. He's promised so much, for me and Trinity…"

"Yeah, but if Trinity is right, do you really want a murderer for a mayor?" Zack challenged.

She sighed. Trinity tugged on her sleeve and held up the cross again for Stephanie to take. The clasp wasn't broken, she saw, it had just come undone. She replaced it on her neck and held onto the cross tightly.

"All right. I'll go find this place," she said finally.

"I'll go with you. It could be dangerous," Ellie offered.

"No, I'm going by myself."

"But there are guys. They'll try and kill you," Zack protested.

"I don't want you going and getting hurt," George said.

"Wiley won't hurt me…if it really is him that's behind this," Stephanie said emphatically. "Just…let me do this."

George shook his head and rubbed his hand over his receding hairline. "If you're not back within a half-hour, I'm going out after you."

Stephanie nodded, her head reeling with too much information for her to swallow. She kissed Trinity on the forehead, and then squeezed past George, Zack and Ellie. She didn't look back as she hurried down the stairs, grabbing her purse and a sweater, and then hurried outside.

Halfway down Duncan Street she regretted not changing her shoes, but she didn't want to head back now. This would be easy. She'd walk onto the Commons—safe at night because Wiley had made it safe!—and not find the stupid trap door. Where was it, the centre of the Commons? She laughed and shook her head. You would think that after all the rowdy concerts and other events held on there that someone would've already discovered it.

After ten minutes of walking and toe-pinching agony, Stephanie made it to the edge of Canada's oldest urban park. There was no one in sight, and the street lamps cast an eerie light on the grass that made the place seem almost otherworldly. She felt like Alice, wandering into a strange nightly Wonderland as she stepped onto the grass.

Now that she thought about it, Wiley never did tell her much about his evenings. Sure, she'd spent many of them with him at rallies, fundraisers and dinners, but after that...she had no idea. He had always asked questions about her days, her weekends. And come to think of it, why was he using his cell phone to talk to his family long distance, assuming that they did really live out west? That would cost a fortune, and she was sure he was only on a pay-as-you-go plan. Yes, he was, she had set it up herself. Why would he waste precious minutes on a long distance call?

Unless it wasn't really long distance.

Stephanie shivered as a strong breeze blew through the Commons. She wobbled in her heels. Stopping only for a moment, she pried them off her feet and tucked them under her arm. The grass was cold on her soles of her feet, but it was refreshing after walking in those heels all day.

She was about to start again when she caught movement in her left periphery. She whirled around.

"Stephanie," Wiley said. He was dressed in all black and blended in with the night. "What are you doing here?"

She hesitated. "I was about to ask you the same thing."

He put his hands on his hips. "Sometimes I like to stroll through the Commons at night. It's very relaxing."

"Yes," Stephanie said slowly. "Listen, I'm really sorry about Trinity tonight. I shouldn't have brought her. She ruined the event for everyone, tarnished your name—"

"Shh, shh, it's okay," Dalton said, drawing closer to her. "I've taken care of it."

"What...what do you mean?" Stephanie's voice wavered.

He smiled at her. "Stephanie, you know I care for you. Deeply."

Her heart pounded faster in her chest. "Yes, I know."

"And I'm not perfect. I..." He hesitated. "I've been thinking about you for a long time now. In a way that's not right, not fair to George."

"Wiley..."

"I know, please, just hear me out." He cleared his throat. "I want what's best for you, and Trinity. I feel...I feel for her. I want to take care of her, and help you take care of her."

Everything that Zack and Ellie had told her about Wiley being a murderer seemed far away in her mind. All she could see was Wiley's intense green eyes penetrating her, wanting her. Her breath caught and her head spun like she was drunk. She was drunk, on her infatuation with him.

He reached out his with his large, caring hands and caressed her cheek. "You've done so much for me. Let me take care of you, and Trinity."

A single tear rolled down Stephanie's face. She wanted him to envelop her, to take all of the responsibilities away from her. Her breathing was raspy and she didn't know what to do.

"Hold me," she whispered.

Wiley wrapped himself around her, his lips and teeth finding her neck and sending chills down her spine. She melted into him and felt everything float away. Nothing else mattered. She was so caught up in her ecstasy for him that she barely felt the blunt pain that struck her so suddenly on the back of her head.

*

It was Ellie who voiced what everyone was thinking. "We should go after her."

The TV was on in the living room, but no one was paying attention. It was something to cut through the awkward silence that hung in the air. After Stephanie had left, George had grabbed the cordless phone; a pointless effort, Ellie thought, since she wasn't sure if Stephanie even had a cell phone with her. While she sat on the couch, trying to relieve her anxieties by picking at a frayed end of her skirt, Zack paced the room. Back and forth, in front of the TV; it would have made Ellie dizzy if she could bring herself to watch him. He had paced after they'd kissed, too.

Trinity was the real eye of the storm. The drug was on its last legs in her now. She sat next to Ellie on the couch, her back straight as a board. She held the pages of her manuscript to her chest. The back of her hand was smeared with black mascara; Ellie had done her best to wash the rest of it off her face. Zack had tried to fix her something to eat but the peanut butter crackers lay untouched on the coffee table in front of her and Ellie. At least she'd let Ellie help her into some different clothes: a white t-shirt that said CITADEL HIGH and some worn jeans.

George was already at the door, stuffing his feet into his shoes. "She hasn't called...we should have gone earlier."

They all should have gone with Stephanie, Ellie thought. After what had happened to her and Zack on the Commons... and then afterwards, in Zack's basement...

"It's been almost a half-hour," Zack said, checking his watch. "Did she take a cell phone with her?"

"I thought she had one on her," George said, shaking the cordless phone in his hand. "I'll try it…"

While he punched the number into the phone, Trinity laid her story on the coffee table. She treated it as if it were a newborn babe, gently rustling the pages and then straightening them neatly. The piece of paper on top of the stack was half blank. She picked up a black pen gingerly and allowed it to flow freely across the page in perfect, pre-accident Trinity cursive.

Zack knelt before the coffee table. "She's writing!"

George held the phone to his ear as he came briskly and squatted next to Zack. "I'm not getting any answer on the phone."

Trinity suddenly dropped the pen, spilling a few drops of ink on the paper. She pushed the page at Ellie and then ran for the door. Ellie scrambled to read the page while Zack ran to help Trinity with her shoes.

Ellie read it aloud:

It was time. Edmund gazed at Victoria, the chains tightly securing her wrists that connected to a chain on the wall. The Knives gleamed on the slab in front of her. Soon she would see what he had done for her. He would cleanse the world and she would love him for it.

"Stephanie…" George pushed the end button on the phone and dropped it on the floor.

Abandoning the page, Ellie slipped into her heels at the door.

"Wait," George said. He glanced at his daughter. "Trinity, maybe you should stay here. Can you do that? And wait for us to bring Mommy home?"

Ellie was already half way out the door when she stopped. It would be dangerous. Too dangerous for Trinity. They wouldn't be able to look after her. She had barely been able to look after Zack and herself. And if something were to happen to Trinity…

Zack ran a hand through Trinity's hair. "Maybe he's right. You should stay."

Trinity shook her head defiantly. "I…I want…to…come too."

"It will be safer for you here," Ellie said.

But she was already pushing past Ellie, sending a blast of night air onto the porch. George dug his car keys from his pocket as the three of them followed Trinity outside. She waited at the car, staring down the street.

"You'll have to protect her," Zack said, catching Ellie by the arm.

It was dark but she could feel his eyes on her. He hadn't touched her since the other night. He was so warm and Ellie's heart begged for him to pull her in and protect her, but no, that was not going to be the way this went. She had to be strong, like she had always been, and hope that maybe this was the time when he saw her for who she really was, instead of someone he refused to have.

George was waiting for them in the car with Trinity. Zack and Ellie piled into the back. They had barely shut their doors when George revved the engine and backed onto the street.

"If she's not on the Commons, we're calling the police. Got that?" He looked at Zack from the rear-view.

"Yeah." Zack patted his cell phone, safely stowed in his pocket.

Two minutes later they arrived at the edge of the Commons. Ellie checked her watch: almost 11 PM. George parked illegally next to a fire hydrant. They slammed the car doors as they jumped out of the car. Where Edmund had posted guards to torment the pedestrians only a few nights before, the Commons was eerily quiet. No one was about but them.

"Empty…" Trinity observed.

CHAPTER ELEVEN

When Stephanie came to, her wrists ached. It was dark and the air smelt like must, moss, and the earth. She tried to move but her wrists had been chained. They rattled as she struggled against them. Her feet were tied together with rope. There was a dull pain in the back of her head and she tried to remember what happened.

"You're awake."

Wiley's voice was like a strange melody to her ears. She looked up as a ring of torches lit all around the room—no, not a room, a cave. The "ceiling" was twenty feet high, at least. The torchlight faded from bright yellow to red to black the further she looked up. A group of men hidden in giant black robes with a red stripe across the top of the hood stood in a silent vigil around a giant slab of rock in the middle of the cavern. From what Stephanie could tell, the slab was painted red. Somewhere off in the distance, maybe in another cavern, she heard screaming and crying. More prisoners? The thought made her sick. Closer to her was another, smaller rock slab with a series of knives—five of them, lined up neatly from smallest to largest.

She had read this description before. Five knives, just like in the ritual in Trinity wrote about. Her eyes slid back to Wiley, who was wearing an identical black robe, but his hood was down, revealing his true identity.

"Trinity was right," Stephanie whispered.

Wiley—now Edmund—smiled and walked closer to her. "You never told me your daughter was gifted with a psychic ability."

"I...I didn't know," Stephanie replied, rattling her chains. "You never told me you enjoyed murdering innocent people."

"You think I murder the innocent?" Edmund said darkly. He clasped his hands in front of him. The torchlight put half his face in shadow and the other in a terrible red glow; she felt as if she were speaking to the devil himself. "I don't murder. I Redeem those not fit to walk this earth."

"Sounds like murder to me." She gritted her teeth. "I trusted you."

"You know I'd never hurt you, Stephanie," he said softly. He caressed her cheek like he had (hours? minutes?) before. Where once his touch had made her knees buckle, it now felt like ants crawling over her skin. She stared daggers at him, trying to show that she wasn't afraid, but the knives gleaming in the torchlight on the slab made her stomach turn.

"What do you want with me?" she demanded.

Edmund put on his charming smile. It sickened Stephanie that it still made her want him.

"I want you to see the difference I will make when I be-come the mayor," he replied. He gestured to one of his hooded followers. "Brother Linus?"

Linus broke the circle around the centre slab and went out of the only exit, to Stephanie's far left. He returned shortly with four other hooded men, restraining Zack, Ellie, Trinity and George. Ellie and George fought hard against their captors, but George wasn't that tall and the man holding him looked like a football player draped in a black tablecloth. Trinity didn't struggle at all. She stared solemnly ahead, in her comatose-like state, and Zack only had eyes for her.

"Trinity!" Stephanie called out.

Trinity slid her eyes to her, but didn't react, as if she'd expected to see Stephanie like this. "Mommy."

"Honey, are you okay?" George asked.

"I'm fine," she said. "You shouldn't have come."

Edmund sauntered towards the centre slab and extended his hands, palm upward. "I'm glad you did. A nice change of pace. Brother Linus, Brother Stephen, it is time for the first sacrifice."

Linus and the man who held Trinity tugged on her and dragged her towards the blood soaked centre slab. The men surrounding it parted ways to let them through. Only now did Trinity struggle against them.

"No, stop it, take me!" Zack cried.

"You're next, chink, don't worry," Edmund replied.

"Please…please don't hurt her," Stephanie pleaded. "You said you would take care of her."

As soon as the words were out of her mouth, she realized the double meaning behind them. She gaped in horror at the obvious signs that had been in front of her eyes, and her ignorance when seeing them before. Zack and Ellie were right. Wiley—Edmund—was a monster. Sobs escaped her, and she wanted to take one of those knives and drive it into herself for being so horribly and wretchedly stupid.

"Trinity died the moment her fragile brain splattered all over the pavement that rainy night," Edmund said. "She's been a burden to you, Stephanie. She's held you back, threatened your career—"

"I almost made you the mayor!" Stephanie screamed.

"Yes, and you did a very good job," Edmund said, not unkindly. "I'm relieving you of all your responsibilities now. The election will happen, and I will ascend to Mayor. Trinity...I can finish her here. Think: no more hospital trips, no more fees for special education. You and George can spend the rest of your lives, happy without the constant pitter-pattering of her feet, or the scratching of her writing pens." He touched the cross that hung around her neck. "I'm doing you and the world a favour by Redeeming her in the eyes of God."

Linus and Stephen held Trinity down on the slab and started to wrap the chains around her middle.

"God has no eyes," Trinity said quietly.

"He has a mouth," Edmund replied. "He told you to write those nasty things about me, didn't he? Yes, He's quite the talker."

"I listen," Trinity said simply.

She no longer struggled. Linus and Stephen were about to finish chaining her to the rock when Edmund held up his hands. "I want to see her squirm. No chains."

Linus protested. "But if she—"

"Hold her down," Edmund instructed. "The chains will only block her wrists and impede the Fifth Knife's job. Brothers, take your knives."

"No! Stop!" Stephanie cried.

Her words fell on deaf ears. One by one the brethren re-trieved the knives from the slab closest to Stephanie. She rattled her chains and tried to move closer, to stop them, but she nearly fell flat on her face. One of them handed a knife—larger than the others, with a jagged edge on the tip, to Edmund. Edmund admired the knife and then sauntered to a different slab where Stephanie couldn't see clearly.

"Come and receive the offering from Omnus," he said to his men.

*

Ellie had tried, but she had failed.

Edmund's followers had come from thin air and surrounded them before she had a chance to defend herself and her friends. They had no choice but to surrender. And these guys were all so strong; Ellie's arm ached as the hooded brother gripped her tightly. Add that to the residual strain from the flips she'd done the other night, and trudging through the dirt in her uncomfortable heels; Ellie didn't know if she could even deal with a confrontation right now.

As they stepped into the monstrous cavern that Trinity had described in her story, her worst fears were confirmed. Edmund had been waiting for them. Stephanie was chained to the wall like bait, which of course, that was what she'd been. George hadn't struggled much before then but now he was trying to be as slippery as an eel to escape his captor, which was hard for a heavy set man to do against six feet of muscle.

At Edmund's command, all of the brethren save the ones that were holding Ellie, Zack, George and Trinity captive lined up around a flat rock off to the side of the cavern. A line of goblets awaited the eager brethren. Each took one and hurried back to the centre slab, the one stained in various shades of red; Ellie feared that their blood would coat it soon if she didn't do something.

Edmund joined his followers and raised his goblet high above his head.

"Thank you, Omnus, for this offering. Now, let us drink!"

The cup in Ellie's purse, the one that Trinity had drank from earlier...

"Drugged. It's drugged!" Ellie shouted.

They didn't listen. The men gulped down their drinks greedily. Edmund held the rim to his lips and tipped the goblet, but didn't drink as deeply as the other men. He set the goblet on the ground.

"He didn't drink it!" Ellie said.

"The words of the Impure are confused," Edmund said simply. He turned to his men. "Now, ready your knives and open your minds to accept Omnus' power."

Suddenly, Trinity jolted, bringing her legs up and kicking one of the brethren in the face. Another man tried to grab her legs but she kicked them in the jaw. Seizing the opportunity, Ellie rammed her heel into the bare foot of the man who held her captive, and swung around. He was tall and muscled, but Ellie was faster. She kicked him in the stomach, her heel puncturing the fabric of the black robe, and then grabbed onto a tuft of hair sticking out from beneath the hood and brought his head down on the cold, damp stone floor. He groaned and was still, but she didn't have time to see if he was out cold or not. She sprinted around the blood rock, her heart racing as she narrowed in on the man holding the First Knife. He looked overwhelmed—stab Trinity, or deal with the oncoming angry blonde girl? He raised his knife; one hand on Trinity's shoulder. Ellie kneed him in the balls and swerved to avoid the knife.

Edmund grinned. The chaos didn't seem to bother him. Stephanie screamed a warning to Trinity as the man with the First Knife brought the blade down. Trinity rolled to avoid it as he released her, gripping his balls tenderly. The tip of the knife slid across and then bounced off the stone with a chalk-on-chalkboard screeching sound. Trinity found her feet. Before Ellie could move to protect her further, Trinity leapt on Edmund's face.

No one moved to help him. Maybe it was the drugs, but Ellie noticed the hooded brothers wobble in place, some of them using the blooded stone to keep their balance. Ellie was frozen, afraid that she would get in Trinity's way, or afraid that she would hurt Trinity by accident. Wrapping her legs around his middle, Trinity endured as Edmund punched her in the side, once, then twice. Trinity wailed and shoved her index and middle fingers into Edmund's eyes until his eyeballs were nothing but white goo.

"Stab her!" Edmund cried.

It all happened too quickly. The four brothers with knives ploughed through the air like reanimated corpses, bearing their knives like savages. Ellie had to duck or be killed. But it wasn't her they were interested in. The four knives struck Trinity in the back. Stephanie's chains rattled as she screamed for her daughter, but Trinity made no sound. Like a leech that had tasted salt, Trinity released her grip on Edmund and fell to the ground.

The men that held Zack and George let go, and Zack stumbled as he ran for Trinity. No one tried to stop him. The drugged brethren seemed to be in a trance as they gathered around Trinity, watching her blood soak into the earth. Ellie didn't know what to do. She didn't know CPR. The bleeding would have to be stopped. But how? A thousand things raced through Ellie's mind as Zack pushed everyone out of his way and knelt before his dying girlfriend.

Stephanie's cries echoed in the cavern. "My baby...my baby..."

Edmund stood still, his breathing horse, blood pouring out of the black holes where his eyes used to be. "Give me a knife. Finish her and allow her to be Redeemed."

The man who Ellie had kneed in the balls turned a lazy eye to his leader. His speech was slow and deliberate. "Brother

Edmund…we used the sacred knives…wrong order. Won't Omnus…punish…us?"

"Shut up," Edmund growled. "She is the evil that Omnus fears! Finish her!"

He held out his hand and felt for the robe of the nearest man. Instead, his hand found the sharp edge of his knife and gripped it before he realized what it was. Edmund cried out in pain, his wail masked only by Zack's as he cried over Trinity's bleeding body.

"Please don't die," he sobbed. "Please don't…"

The knife. Ellie snatched it from Edmund's flailing fingers. The words "First Knife" were carved into the silver hilt.

"Incompetent fools, finish the chink—"

She positioned behind him, near his heart. Please God, forgive me, she thought, but this man does not deserve to live.

"—allow him to join her in being—"

Just before he could finish his command, Edmund arched his back, his face frozen in pain and surprise. The knife went in easy, like she was stabbing thin air.

So easy to kill.

The thought sickened her as he stumbled backward and slammed into her. She grunted as she pushed him away. Ellie trembled. Her knuckles were white from her grip on the knife. She threw it on the ground with a loud, guilty clatter.

"No…kill them…" Edmund gurgled before slipping into unconsciousness.

There was the faint sound of sirens in the distance that was almost like a death toll for Edmund. When had they called the police? George…must have before they got captured…Ellie leaned against the cave wall. She was starting to see stars.

The sirens must have spooked the brethren. They panicked about being caught and being sent to jail, and together they fled the cave like a flock of ravens, leaving their dying leader alone on the ground.

The sirens…the police would know what she did. That she killed a man. But maybe that was okay, Ellie thought as her eyelids drooped. She did it for Zack. He wasn't even looking at her, but that was okay too. Trinity was safe. That meant Zack was happy, and if he was happy…

*

They sat sombrely in the waiting room, heads bowed, as if they were in church and not a hospital. It was familiar, but not comforting.

The aftermath of what happened in the cavern was a blur. Zack remembered the police coming, and George finding a key to release Stephanie from her chains. He remembered being questioned, but not by who or what he was asked. They all ended up knowing about Wiley Dalton in the end, though. Maybe he'd even blabbed about Trinity's foreknowledge about everything. It wasn't important. Trinity was dying. She and Edmund were rushed to the QEII Hospital, in separate vehicles.

And Ellie…

She was next to him now. Stiff, bruised…but alive. She'd barely said a word to him since…since the kiss. Not real words. And yet, she'd saved them all.

Trinity was in surgery for hours. Zack stayed in the waiting room with George and Ellie, but Stephanie had run back home to fetch Trinity's manuscript. The police wanted it, she said. As evidence.

And when Ellie mentioned the empty poisoned cup of orange juice she'd hidden in her purse, a look crossed

Stephanie's face that was part guilt, and part surprise.

Zack was grateful to Ellie for that, too.

Twenty-four long hours later, the four of them were still at the hospital. Outside, the world was buzzing: Edmund was dropped from the election. The media ran stories on rumours that he was involved in a Satanist cult, while others proposed he was the victim of brainwashing. Some newspapers did some digging and speculated he was connected to a string of violent, ritualistic murders out west. He read it all on his phone until his eyes hurt. It would take a few days to get everything cleared up, Stephanie said. Dr. Letofsky appeared in the hallway, holding a clipboard. "Hartell family?"

Stephanie stood, holding George's hand tightly. Zack and Ellie followed.

"How is she, Doctor?" Stephanie asked.

"She'll live," Dr. Letofsky replied. He flipped through the pages attached to the clipboard. "Massive internal bleeding, one of the wounds was near her heart. Another barely missed her spinal cord. But she seems to be recovering well."

"Will she be able to go to the prom?" Zack asked; he knew the answer as soon as he spoke.

"I don't know how she'll be up for that," Dr. Letofsky said with a sympathetic look. "But her recovery the first time was miraculous, so we'll see." He cleared his throat and continued. "There's also something else I'd like to show you, and I'm afraid the news is not as pleasant. Mr. and Ms. Hartell, if you wouldn't mind-?"

"Zack and Ellie can come too," Stephanie declared. She rested a hand on Zack's shoulder. Her wrists were still red from the manacles. "If it weren't for them, Trinity wouldn't be alive right now."

He glanced at Ellie, but her face was pale and made of stone. Dr. Letofsky led the four of them to Trinity's recovery room. She lay awake under a light blue wool blanket that covered everything but her arms and head. Zack had heard from the initial reports from the nurses that she was bandaged from her chest to her pelvis. He pursed his lips. Her eyes drooped sleepily, probably from the medication, but she smiled at him. Returning her smile, he snagged the seat next to the bed and caressed her hand. Tiny scrapes lined her palm and he kissed every one.

Ellie leaned against the wall opposite Trinity with her arms folded, while George and Stephanie stood on the other side of the bed. Stephanie ran her fingers through Trinity's tangled hair. "How are you, sweetie?"

"Mmm…" She turned her head groggily to face her mother. A little bit of drool escaped the corner of her lips. Slowly and deliberately, she wiped it on the back of her hand. "Sleepy."

The doctor unclipped two CT scans from his clipboard. Zack pushed in his chair as Dr. Letofsky walked behind him and slapped one of the scans on a board above Trinity's hospital bed.

"The first scan was the one I took after the accident. And then…"

He put up the other CT scan next to the first. The noticeable difference between the two was that the more recent scan had a large light blue spot in the right side of her brain.

"The second was two weeks ago, when she came in for her follow-up," Dr. Letofsky said. "She has a tumour in the right hemisphere of her brain."

A cold, quiet fear seized Zack's heart as he squeezed Trinity's fingers. This was it, he knew. The news wasn't much worse than learning that she would never be normal again, but he'd never thought that could be true either. That little blue spot on the CT scan was more than just a smudge of ink on a piece of paper. It was real. She'd been so lucky the last few times…maybe…just maybe…

Ellie was at his side, leaning against his chair. He brought Trinity's hand to his forehead. He wouldn't cry. He had to be strong.

"How dangerous is it?" Stephanie asked.

"She may only have a few weeks. A month, maybe." Dr. Letofsky's voice was soft. Soothing. But so was Trinity's warm hand against Zack's skin.

"It could be removed," the doctor continued.

"What are the risks in that?" George asked.

"Well…the tumour is large," Dr. Letofsky admitted. "At the rate it's developing, she'd have to go into surgery tomorrow. But she may not survive the procedure."

"What are the odds?" Zack whispered. His lips were trembling against Trinity's fingers.

The doctor hesitated before replying. "About…twenty-five percent."

The room was silent with dread, save the sound of Trinity's raspy breathing. A tear escaped Zack's eye and fell onto Trinity's palm. He looked up at her but she was gazing at her mother. Stephanie's eyes were watering. She clutched the front of George's shirt like a lifeline. Trinity's lips parted slowly.

"Mommy…s'okay," she said.

Stephanie knelt by Trinity's bedside. "No, it's not okay, sweetie."

"Is okay," she repeated.

Wiping her eye with her thumb, Stephanie refused to give up. "What can we do for you, Trinity? Tell me, and I will do anything to make sure you have what you want."

Dr. Letofsky cleared his throat. "I suggest that you and Mr. Hartell make the decision. Trinity may not have the mental capacity to understand what is best for her."

Stephanie fingered the delicate cross around her neck. "Tumour or God, Doctor, she saved us all. It will be whatever she wants it to be. And we will all live with that." She cast fierce teary-eyed glances at both Zack and Ellie.

Trinity swallowed and drew in a deep breath through her mouth. Her voice was barely above a whisper. "Let me go."

Zack slowly released her hand, but she reached for him again. He took her back, confused. "I don't—"

"Let me…go," she repeated, squeezing his hand as tight as her weakened state would allow.

Zack swallowed a sob. "Go where, Trin?"

But Zack already knew. It was the tumour, it was divine—maybe both. Whatever it was, it was taking her away from him. While his stomach was in knots and he felt like his world was fraying at the edges, she was smiling. She looked so peaceful, so sure of herself. I will visit her every day, he thought.

And for the briefest of seconds, he glimpsed the real Trinity flickering beneath her eyes.

EPILOGUE

The evening was cool and the air was brisk around him. He kept his hands in his pockets for warmth. Just one more minute, he told himself. The sky was already turning shades of purple and red, and the stone markers cast long shadows on the grass. He stood at one of them. It was rounded at the top, and sparkled with tiny, ornate gems that were embedded in the stone. Her name was carved in imposing block letters.

Trinity Lauren Hartell. Seventeen years old. A gift to us all.

Zack did not cry. The day they'd lowered her into the ground, dressed in white with flowers in her hair—that was the hardest. But he'd promised himself he wouldn't. Beneath his black dress shoes, the earth was still fresh from her burial. The grass would claim it soon.

He kneeled and placed a bouquet of roses at the foot of her grave. The knee in his dress pants was getting soiled, but if that was the only piece of her that he could take to prom, then so be it. Other flowers and cards from family and friends and other people that had heard about her story surrounded the stone. Once the investigation into Wiley Dalton had gotten underway, and the news about Trinity's story had leaked to the press, interested publishing companies had contacted Stephanie and George about taking a look at the manuscript. They hadn't decided who to trust it with yet, but Zack was pretty sure they both agreed it had to be published. You are an author, in death, he thought.

A car door shut in the distance. Ellie had probably gotten tired of waiting. He stood and brushed some of the dirt from his knee when she appeared at his side.

She was lovely, radiant even in her purple strapless dress. The cuts and bruises from last week had almost faded and were unnoticeable under her dress and makeup. Long white gloves adorned Ellie's arms up to her elbows, and white shoes peeked out from under her dress. Her dusty blonde hair was pinned back with butterfly clips to reveal more of her face. She had little freckles on her nose. Zack hadn't noticed that before. That with the green grass, the contrast with the purple and the sky… he felt like drawing her.

"I don't want to rush you," she said hesitantly, "but we should probably go soon."

"Yeah…I know." He reached into his pocket and pulled out a rectangular black box. He'd wanted to give it to Trinity before…*before*, but it was more delicate than she was. The box opened on gold hinges and Ellie stepped closer to see.

"She would have really liked it," she said.

A smile touched his lips. The bracelet was a series of small, sapphire hearts. He imagined it on her wrist, imagined her smile, her smell…and then shut the box.

He knelt again and dug a hole big enough, and placed the box inside. Gripping the stone, he bowed his head and mouthed words so that Ellie would not hear. *I'll always love you. Thank you for being with me. I will keep you in my heart, always. Anata wa utsukushii. I don't want to leave...but you were strong, so I will be too.*

He took a deep breath in and stood up. A gentle breeze kissed him and wrapped around his body, urging him on. It was time to go.

Ellie was waiting some distance away, her heels sinking into the soft grass. Zack caught up with her and gave her a hand to steady herself. She accepted it gratefully, her face glowing.

He held out his elbow. "Shall we?"

She beamed at him, and together, they went.

Acknowledgements & Thanks

Mom, Dad, Jessie and family for supporting my writing and publishing.

Brittney. You never stop believing in me.

My classmates in the 2010 Creative Book Publishing Program at Humber College. Without this program I wouldn't know half the things I do about the industry; I'm glad I went through it all with you. You guys are awesome.

A special shout-out to the 3 Day Novel Contest, since if it didn't exist, I wouldn't have written this book.

Helen Marshall(of no relation!), my editor, for helping me expand on my three-day madness.

All of my friends & followers on Twitter. You encourage & inspire me to write when I need to!

And of course, Dave, designer of my beautiful cover & my loving partner. We are beans and rice, forever.

About the Author

Clare C. Marshall grew up in rural Nova Scotia with very little television and dial up internet, and yet, she turned out okay. She has a combined honours in journalism and psychology from the University of King's College, and is a graduate from Humber College's Creative Book Publishing Program. She founded Woulds & Shoulds Editing and Design in 2010 for self-published authors looking for quality editing and design services. When she's not writing, she enjoys playing the fiddle and making silly noises at cats. Within is her first published novel. Follow her on Twitter: @ClareMarshall13.

If you enjoyed this book, please consider posting a review on your blog, or on Amazon. Thank you!

Made in the USA
Charleston, SC
15 April 2016